D1176044

SWIMMING ACROSS THE HUDSON

Joshua Henkin

G. P. PUTNAM'S SONS
New York

This novel is a work of fiction. Any references to historical events; to real people, living or dead; or to real locales are intended only to give the fiction a sense of reality and authenticity. Names, characters, places, and incidents either are the product of the author's imagination or are used fictitiously, and their resemblance, if any, to real-life counterparts is entirely coincidental.

Published by G. P. Putnam's Sons
Publishers Since 1838
200 Madison Avenue
New York, NY 10016
Published simultaneously in Canada

The text of this book is set in Goudy.

Library of Congress Cataloging-in-Publication Data

Henkin, Joshua.
Swimming across the Hudson / Joshua Henkin.
p. cm.
ISBN 0-399-14116-2
I. Title.
PS3558.E49594 1997 96-41235 CIP
813'.54—dc20

Printed in the United States of America
1 3 5 7 9 10 8 6 4 2

This book is printed on acid-free paper. ♾

Book design by Marysarah Quinn

I am grateful to the following people for their assistance: Andrea Brott, Armin Brott, Jason Dubow, Miles Ehrlich, Anna Jardine, and Abby Rose. I'm especially appreciative of Lisa Bankoff, Laura Gaines, and Faith Sale for all that they have done on my behalf.

Thanks finally to The Heekin Group Foundation and the Avery Hopwood and Jule Hopwood Fund for their financial support.

To my parents,
Alice and Louis Henkin,
and my brothers,
David and Daniel

SWIMMING ACROSS THE HUDSON

PART I

There's a story I was told when I was a child.

My parents had friends who lived in Kansas. Their name was Millstein, and I pictured them clearly, swarthy and slow-afoot in the cornfield sun, a Jewish family camped in the heartland.

We lived in New York City and were more Jewish than the Millsteins. That is what my father said: more Jewish, less Jewish, my father always quantifying things, spinning out the lessons that would shape my life. "They *care* about being Jewish," he said, "but what do you do with all that caring?"

My parents did this: They sent my brother, Jonathan, and me to Jewish day school; they kept a kosher home. On Friday nights my mother lit the sabbath candles. She placed her hands across her eyes and said a blessing to the sabbath queen.

I liked the scent of the sabbath, the perfume on my mother's wrists, my father's dress shirts bleached and ironed. I could smell the challah in the kitchen, the marigolds, red and yellow, arranged in their vase. I stood next to Jonathan with my hands behind my back and watched the candles flicker. We wore navy slacks and white oxford shirts, the two of us like twins with our hair slicked back, wearing matching clothes for the sabbath.

My mother had been born Jewish but grew up in a secular home. Her parents sent her to the Ethical Culture School and to summer work camp, where the kids stood in a circle before going to bed and sang "The International."

"Mom's seen some weird things," my father said once. My mother had studied anthropology in college, and had spent time in Bali after she graduated.

She smiled. "I've seen some weird things right inside this apartment."

My father wanted Jonathan and me to be like him—to keep kosher and observe the sabbath, to pepper our conversations with the words of the Torah, the way his father and grandfather had done, generations of Jews speaking the same language, stretching back to Moses.

"Think about that," my father said. "All Jews are related to Moses."

My mother agreed to keep a kosher home even though she didn't believe in God. She learned a little Hebrew; she went to synagogue on the holidays. She liked ritual, she said, and that pleased my father. When we grew up, she told us, we could live as we wanted.

My father knew we'd live as we wanted. But I worried about what would happen if God spoke to him. In synagogue on Rosh Hashanah, we read about the binding of Isaac. I saw Abraham and Isaac in the land of Moriah, a butcher knife gleaming in Abraham's hand.

"Would you do that to me?" I asked my father.

"Don't be silly," he said.

"What if God commanded you?"

"That's impossible. God doesn't speak directly to people anymore."

"He could start to."

"He won't, Ben. It's a counterfactual."

"It's a counterfactual?"

"Right. It's counter to the facts."

Still, I worried. I pictured us in Riverside Park, my father and me on a hill, the kids on their sleds flying by us. Above us hung the trees, windblown and bare, and above them the heavens. I imagined my father holding a knife. He stood next to me with his eyes closed, listening patiently for God's command.

He taught Jonathan and me how to chant from the Torah. We learned prophets and Talmud; we read from "Ethics of the Fathers" after sabbath lunch. On the way to synagogue we conjugated Hebrew verbs, the three of us together keeping beat. Sometimes my mother would join us—*amartee, amarta, amar, amarnu, amartem, amru*—the four of us marching along Riverside Drive, one-two, one-two, the way my father had marched many years before, when he'd fought the Germans in World War II.

The Millsteins, though, were undereducated. They went to synagogue just on Yom Kippur, in a city an hour from their home. They lived in a town of three thousand people where they were the only Jews.

My father looked at Jonathan and me. He was a tall man—taller than I imagined I'd ever be—and I was sure he understood the world.

"Do you know what synagogue is like in Kansas?"

I shook my head.

"It's like church," he said.

"They pray to Jesus," said Jonathan.

"No," my father said, "they don't pray to Jesus, but the services are in English and no one knows what's going on. The cantor faces the congregants and sings to them. It's like a performance."

"Like the opera," Jonathan said.

"Exactly," said my father.

The Millstein boys had had bar mitzvahs, but they weren't bar mitzvahs as we knew them. They were more bar than mitzvah, my father said.

"What does that mean?" my mother asked.

"It means everyone got drunk," I said.

"It was an excuse for a party," said my father.

The Millsteins gave money to the United Jewish Appeal. They

bought Israel Bonds and planted trees in the Negev and had a portrait of Golda Meir hanging in their living room. But this was cultural Judaism, my father said; it wouldn't protect them.

"Protect them from what?" I asked.

"From intermarriage," he said. "From Kansas."

For this was the heart of my father's story. Peter, the Millsteins' eldest son, graduated from college and took a trip around the world. He backpacked through Asia and North Africa, and ended up in Israel, where he worked on a kibbutz, picking melons in the fields. This pleased his parents—their son the Zionist, tilling the soil. They felt fortunate, they said, Peter in a country with all these Jewish girls, and now he might marry within the faith.

But he didn't, my father said. Even in Israel he found a non-Jew—a Swedish girl who worked on the kibbutz—and a year later they got married.

For several seconds my father just stared at us. Then he said, "Do you see my point?"

He was a smart man. He taught political science at Columbia University; he spoke Russian, Italian, German, and French. At night I would find him reading in the living room—books about countries whose names I didn't know, about abstract painting and French literature, about memory, personality, and the workings of the brain. He was a genius, I thought, but I didn't see his point. Marrying a Swede had nothing to do with Kansas.

But I didn't tell him that. And over time, I forgot about the Millsteins.

Then, twelve years later, I too graduated from college and took a trip. I was with a friend driving west, and I called my parents when we got to Kansas. I wanted the Millsteins' phone number.

My father sounded nervous on the other end of the line. "Please, Ben," he whispered, "don't do this."

"Don't do what?"

"Just please don't call them."

I was standing at a pay phone along the edge of the highway; I watched a stream of trucks drive by. And it occurred to me then, in this town I'd never been to, that all these years my father had lied to me. I pictured the Millsteins: hoe in hand, dreidel in pocket, Eastern Europe come to the Dust Bowl. But I could hear it in his voice, the Millsteins weren't real. They were nothing but a lesson.

I'm thirty-one years old now. I live in San Francisco with Jenny and her daughter, Tara; Jonathan lives a mile away from us. Sometimes from my balcony on a clear afternoon I imagine I can see his house.

Jonathan and I are adopted. It's something we've always known, as much a part of us as our bodies, what we have been and always will be. For a while we were embarrassed, for a while we were proud, for a long time Jonathan has been indifferent. Throughout it all my parents considered us their children, said they loved us no less for how we'd arrived.

But last year, without warning, I got a letter from my birth mother. Since then everything has changed.

Sometimes, even now, I think about the Millsteins. I try to remember the things my father taught us, the prayers he said, his wishes for our lives. But Jenny isn't Jewish, and Jonathan is gay, and I see my father in our old apartment, asking my mother where he went wrong, how things might have been different.

I'm only five months older than Jonathan. We were in the same nursery school class. We were in the same class in Jewish day school from kindergarten through twelfth grade. We were in the same class at Yale, where we arrived in September 1982, our dorms facing each other across Old Campus.

This is the story my parents told us: I came along first, but then Jonathan came too, and they took us both because each of us was beautiful.

I liked that story. I liked picturing my parents searching through hospitals, combing the wards filled with babies. I liked imagining the moment they brought us home. I liked pretending that adoption was their first choice, that they didn't want their own children.

But the truth was different.

For several years my mother had tried to get pregnant, and when she finally did, she miscarried. I was nine when she told me this.

"I'm sorry," I said.

"Sorry about what?"

"I'm sorry I killed the baby."

"You didn't kill the baby. You weren't even born. Besides, it wasn't a baby yet. It couldn't have survived."

My room was across the hall from Jonathan's. At night, from our beds, we whispered to each other through a telephone we'd fashioned, a long length of cord between two paper cups. "I killed Frances," I said.

"Who's Frances?"

"The dead baby."

After school, we stood against Jonathan's bedroom wall and measured how tall we were. Jonathan got on tiptoe and fluffed up his hair; he pretended he was taller than I was. Then we played zoo. I placed him inside a laundry basket, and through the mesh of orange plastic fed him Froot Loops one by one. When we were done playing, I told him that we were brothers by birth, that we'd come from the same family.

"That's impossible," he said. "We're too close in age."

"No we're not." I opened *The Guinness Book of World Records* and showed him a picture of the smallest surviving infant, a baby so shriveled it looked like a fig; you couldn't tell it was human. "That's you," I said. "You were born premature."

"No I wasn't."

"We were adopted together. We were a package deal."

"You're lying," Jonathan said.

"They put you in an oven until you were done."

"Like a piece of meat?"

"Like a brisket."

Earlier that year, I'd begun to take karate. One night I came home from school, put on my *gi*, and ran about the apartment making grunting noises, flailing at the furniture.

"Ha-ya!" I shouted.

"You're a white belt," Jonathan said. "You can't break anything."

I karate-chopped his bureau. I hit it with both hands again and again, until my palms turned red and my skin grew tender and the pain was too much for me to bear.

"You're crazy," he said.

"We're adopted."

"So what?"

"So self-defense is important."

I went into my parents' bedroom, where I found my mother's

sewing kit. I returned to Jonathan's room a minute later with a needle. I pricked my left index finger, and a drop of blood welled up. I pricked my middle finger too. Then I handed the needle to Jonathan.

"What are you doing?" he asked.

"It's a blood pact. It's our promise to protect each other."

In school I'd learned about the power of blood, how lineage was everything in Jewish law. I watched the men in synagogue chant from the Torah, Shmuel the son of Zvi, Yosef the son of Peretz, the Levites and Israelites, everything going back to Mount Sinai. Where, I wondered, did I fit in all this? Where did Jonathan fit?

"Am I Jewish?" I asked my father.

"Of course you are."

"But was I *born* Jewish?"

"Yes," he said. "Jonathan too."

Still, I didn't know where I came from. I'd read about kidnappings, children abducted from their homes, their organs removed and donated to science.

"I might have been kidnapped and given to you," I said.

"You weren't," said my father. "Trust me."

"What if I get kidnapped now?"

"You won't."

"It happened to Patty Hearst."

"Patty Hearst was kidnapped by some nuts who said they were political, but all they wanted was her father's money. No one's interested in our money."

But at night, through our telephone, I told Jonathan to be on guard. "Watch out for kidnappers," I said. I pulled on the cord to make sure he was holding the other end. "Be strong and loyal. Always keep an eye on who's behind you."

He came out to me our sophomore year of college. It was a Saturday night. We were about to see *Everything You Always Wanted to Know About Sex but Were Afraid to Ask*. Jonathan spoke to me as the lights started to dim, hoping, it seemed, to break the news without giving me a chance to react.

"I'm gay," he said.

I'd suspected the truth, but now that I'd heard it, I felt oddly disappointed. In summer camp, as teenagers, we'd made out with our girlfriends in adjoining pagodas; we'd once dated identical twins. Already I missed that bond we'd had, that teenage tie of hormones and discovery, of growing up together.

"You're my brother," I said. "That's the only thing that matters to me."

But throughout the movie I thought about his news. I imagined the moment he'd tell our parents, the instant everything would change. I could see them in the middle of the night, gray-haired and spent, in faded pajamas, numb, cast-off, sleepless.

On the screen before us, Gene Wilder was in love with a sheep.

"You can tell Mom and Dad that," I said.

"What?"

"Tell them you're in love with a sheep." I reached into the box of popcorn, where Jonathan's hand was. The touch of his fingers startled me. "Then tell them the truth. It will sound good by comparison."

At brunch the next day, I asked him whether he had a boyfriend.

He did, he said. His name was Sandy.

"How long have you two been going out?"

"Since Thanksgiving."

"Thanksgiving? That's almost three months ago. You should have told me. I'd have understood."

He didn't answer me.

"Was Sandy your first?"

"My what?"

"You know. The first guy you slept with."

"There have been a few others."

"A few? What does that mean? Three? Twenty?"

"It's none of your business. I don't ask how many girls you've slept with."

This was early 1984. AIDS was in the news. I reached across the table and touched Jonathan's hand. "You could die."

"You could too. Straight people get AIDS also. Besides, I can take care of myself."

His gaze was blank. He seemed to be staring right through me, toward somewhere, something, I couldn't understand.

A month later, in March, he came out to my parents by mail. Before sending his note, he showed me what he'd written, wanting to know what I thought.

Dear Mom and Dad,

I'm gay. I have a boyfriend. His name is Sandy. I don't want to have to hide this from you.

Love,
Jonathan

The note was written on a postcard, oddly public for what he was telling them. Everyone read other people's postcards. He was coming out to the mailman; he was coming out to my parents' next-door neighbors, to the world. On the front of the postcard was a picture of a boy balanced on the railing of a sandbox. Jonathan had done that as a child, walking along the Riverside Park sandbox railing across the street from our home. Was he sending my parents a message, telling them that he was still the boy he'd been?

"Talk to them," I said. "It would be better that way."

"I can't. I'm too afraid."

"You can try."

I'd always thought of us as related, assumed that whatever I felt he did too. Now I realized this wasn't so. We looked different from each other, more so than ever. He was taller and ganglier than I was, all elbows and knees. His skin was darker than mine, his eyes lighter. The whiskers were thick on his upper lip and chin, while I could still go a week without shaving. He'd become a leader in the movement to divest from South Africa. Sometimes at night I'd see him camped inside a shanty.

"They'll still love you," I said, staring at the postcard.

"I'm not sure."

"They will. Believe me."

Perhaps this had to do with his being adopted. If he'd been born to them, he might have been more confident that they would love him for who he was, that he was their son and they wouldn't trade him.

"I wish they could find out by accident," he said. "Maybe I'll fly to Europe and write them from there. I need to put an ocean between us."

How long, I wondered, had he known he was gay? I wanted to ask him, but I was afraid—afraid he'd say it wasn't my business, afraid he'd tell me he'd always known and all these years he'd been faking it.

My mother wrote back before my father did. Jonathan showed me her letter, as if trying to include me in the correspondence.

Dear Jonathan,

We love you. That's most important. We hope you'll call us when you're ready. I was surprised by the news, but if this is who you are and you're sure of it, then I want you to know you have my support and I'll always stand up for you. You're our babies—you and Ben both. Nothing will ever change that.

Love,
Mom

My mother grew more adamant as the weeks passed, trying to demonstrate her support for Jonathan. She sent him magazine clippings about gay adult children and their parents; she went to the library and read gay fiction. It seemed to me that she was trying too hard. Sometimes I see this even now, my mother always doing what's right, as if this were another cause to fight for, pretending she isn't ambivalent about this—my mother who dreamed Jonathan would get married, who used to talk to us about grandchildren.

We're a family of letter-writers, and my mother wrote me too.

Dear Ben,

Jonathan told us he's gay. Dad and I will do our best to be there for him. But we're worried. We read about AIDS all the time. We'd like to say something to him, but Dad doesn't know how to, and I'm not sure what to say either. Maybe you can say something to him—if you feel comfortable.

Love,
Mom

I spoke to her a few days later, but I said nothing about her comment on AIDS, and I didn't mention that I'd already spoken to Jonathan. I refused to talk behind his back. I didn't want to be their intermediary.

When my father wrote Jonathan, he was more reticent than my mother. He danced around the subject of my brother's coming out. He was working on an article about 1950s Soviet culture, and he described the research he was doing and asked Jonathan about his work. He wrote about the social safety net and the mean-spiritedness of the Reagan budget cuts. But he only briefly mentioned Jonathan's announcement. "You shouldn't jump to any conclusions," his letter read. "You're still young and trying to figure things out. College is an exciting time, but a lot of what you think when you're in college won't mean anything twenty years from now."

"Dad believes this is just a phase," Jonathan said.

"Give him time," I told him. "He'll come to terms with it eventually."

Every letter my father sent us had the Hebrew date on top and the words "with the help of God," written in Hebrew, in the upper right-hand corner. Sometimes he declared his love to us in Hebrew. He liked to allude to verses in the Torah, to remind us of everything the three of us shared. But this letter to Jonathan, more than others, was filled with such verses. Perhaps my father was being indirect, reminding Jonathan that the Torah prohibited him from having sex with another man.

That's what Jonathan thought. He said my father would use the Torah against him.

"I doubt it," I said. "Dad's too uncomfortable to confront you. You know how he hates to talk about sex."

"But I'm his son. He cares what I do. And he believes in God. For all I know, he really thinks God gave the Torah to Moses. It's hard to figure out what Dad believes."

"You know what Dad believes."

"Not really. His life is the university. That's who he is. But then he gets up every morning and prays to God."

"He loves you," I said. "That's what counts."

But was I being honest? Was I so concerned about protecting Jonathan that I wasn't willing to admit that I too was disappointed, that I'd hoped we'd grow up and be larger versions of ourselves, that we'd marry sisters and live across the street from each other, that because we were adopted nothing could separate us?

When we came home for summer break, my father spoke directly to Jonathan. He didn't say anything about religion. He just wanted to know who Sandy was.

"He's a guy, Dad. What else do you want me to tell you? He's tall. He grew up in New Mexico."

"Where did you meet him?"

"In anthropology class. What difference does it make?"

"I just want to know what he's like."

For this was what my father thought: that Sandy had made Jonathan gay. My father was a decent man, but he convinced himself that, if not for Sandy, Jonathan would have gone out with a nice Jewish girl and settled down and married.

"What would you have done if you'd gone to Harvard?" my father asked him.

"The same thing I'm doing right now. I'd be sleeping in a dorm room and going to class. I'd be living my life, only in Cambridge."

"You wouldn't have met Sandy, and everything that followed would have been different."

"I'd have met someone else."

"She might have been a girl."

"There are lots of girls at Yale."

At night, the first week we were home, my father sat in the living room, reading books about psychological development and the inner workings of the human brain. He got recommendations from professors in Columbia's psychology department and brought home library books by genetic determinists and radical behaviorists, and laid them out in two piles as if to weigh them against each other. He'd been first in his class in high school and college and had always believed he could understand the world if only he read enough pages. But he didn't understand what was happening to Jonathan. This boy who for years had gone with him to synagogue had become someone he didn't know.

"Dad," I said one night, "you should try to get some sleep." The two of us were alone in the living room.

"I'm all right," he said.

I stared at the books at his feet. He covered them when Jonathan was around, like a teenager hiding pornography. But Jonathan knew what he was reading.

"You could read something else," I suggested. "Try a novel, or a book of poetry."

"What's more important than my children?"

Your children are all right, I wanted to tell him. But I didn't say anything.

My mother tried to talk sense to him. She was persuasive and intelligent. She'd gone to Yale Law School for a year, then dropped out to become a union organizer. For seven years she tended to Jonathan and me full-time, then went back to work, as an advocate for the homeless. She lobbied for funding at City Hall and in Albany; she helped people get medical treatment and legal counsel; she worked with soup kitchen administrators; she organized media campaigns for public support. One time she even got my father to agree to let a homeless person spend the night in our living room.

My father was a formal man. He didn't think living rooms were meant for sleeping in, whether you were homeless or not. He wore a suit to work every day, and he refused to eat even an ice cream cone in the street. He reminded Jonathan and me what "Ethics of the Fathers" said: Dogs eat in the street; people don't. But he agreed to let a homeless man stay in our apartment because he loved my mother. She could get him to do things that no one else could.

Now she was arguing with him about Jonathan, trying to persuade him to accept who my brother was.

"I just want him to be happy," my father said.

"I do too." My mother was silent for a moment. "Maybe this will make him happy."

"It's a hard world. He'll spend his whole life confronting other people's prejudices."

"Let's not make it any harder." My mother still had her law casebooks, which she occasionally removed from the closet and quoted from to my father. Sexual orientation, she was telling him, was like race twenty years ago. This was the issue her children would hold her responsible for.

"It's different," my father said.

"What's different about it?"

"It just is."

She quoted to him from *Plessy v. Ferguson*.

"What's your point?"

"This is what people used to think. Decent people, like you and me."

"*Plessy* is about segregation," he said. "I'm not talking about segregation. I'm talking about our baby. We brought him up as if he were our own."

"He *is* our own."

"I know that."

Over the years he has accommodated to her point of view. Although he still gets uncomfortable when he sees Jonathan and Sandy touch, he does his best to be respectful.

But Jonathan remembered that my father thought Sandy had made him gay. He poked fun at my father. "If you hadn't gone to Yeshiva University, who knows what would have happened? You might have met a nice guy."

"Don't be silly," my father said. "I'd still have met Mom, because we were meant for each other. God was watching over me."

The following Passover, our junior year of college, Jonathan brought Sandy home. Sandy was the first person in his family to attend college; before going to Yale he'd never met a Jew. He had come out while in high school, although no one else in his hometown was openly gay.

If he'd suffered from culture shock when he first got to Yale, it was no longer apparent. He had friends on campus and in the New Haven gay community. He'd won the freshman composition prize. Like my brother, he was active in the divestment movement. Now, at our seder, he was doing well, sitting between Jonathan and my mother, reading from the Haggadah in transliterated Hebrew and asking my father questions about the text.

Why, Sandy wanted to know, was enslavement in Egypt the formative Jewish story? What about the Spanish Inquisition or the Holocaust? Weren't they more tragic and therefore more important? Perhaps Jonathan had coached Sandy. Perhaps Sandy had guessed how to win my father's heart, by being an interested student.

"I've wondered that myself," my father said. "Why harp on Egypt so many years later? But it's less what happened in Egypt than what happened afterward—Mount Sinai and the giving of the Torah. Before the Exodus, the Jews weren't a people. They were simply the Israelites, the Eevreem. But in the desert they were given the Torah. That's what transformed them into a nation before God. Egypt was the beginning of this process."

Framed photographs of Justices Brandeis and Frankfurter, my father's heroes when he was young, hung on the dining room walls. Above my mother's head, facing the Hudson River, were bookshelves built into the wall. I'd once counted the books on them; there were more than five hundred. Who else had books even in the dining room? What could Sandy make of this?

We had a matzo sandwich with horseradish and *haroset*, the horseradish to commemorate the pains of slavery. We ate a full meal, and for dessert had kosher-for-Passover seven-layer cake made from potato flour. Finally we ate the *afikoman*, which we'd hidden at the beginning of the seder.

"This is the real dessert," my father said. "It's better than seven-layer cake."

Then we said Grace after Meals. Sandy stayed quiet, with his head bowed. Jonathan and I had stopped being religious our freshman year of college; my parents knew that. But when I came home, I acted as if everything were the same. I went to synagogue with my father; I celebrated the sabbath in my parents' home. Jonathan didn't approve of this. You shouldn't pray, he said, to someone you don't believe in. Now, though, at the seder, he was singing along. I was singing too, happy to see that we were a family again.

My mother asked Sandy about his childhood. Had he spent his whole life in New Mexico? Had his parents come to visit him at Yale?

"They've never been east of the Mississippi," Sandy said. "They'd like to come, but it's expensive." Sandy's father owned a repair shop and didn't want to leave it unattended. Sandy's parents had never been on an airplane, and Sandy suspected they were afraid of flying. Here he was, the classic story: the boy who goes to college and leaves everything behind, who can never come home again.

Jonathan's and Sandy's hands touched. What exactly did I feel? Was it mere discomfort? For my parents? For myself? Or was it envy, really, that Sandy had taken my brother away from me? Walking down Riverside Drive when we were small, we used to hold hands. When we were a little older, we lay on the same bed late at night and watched the Knicks on TV, disregarding our parents' orders to go to sleep. Now we were in college, and we rarely touched.

When dinner was over, my mother put sheets and towels in the guest bedroom, where Sandy would spend the night. That was the rule—girlfriends, and now boyfriends, stayed in separate bedrooms. My mother pretended this was my father's policy, but it was really hers also. She had us believe that she was liberated, but she didn't like to think about her sons having sex.

Still, she left a condom on Jonathan's nightstand.

"Mom," I said, holding it up. "This is embarrassing."

"What is? He needs to protect himself."

I thought of saying something about the letter she'd sent me. But what? That it wasn't her business? That she should leave Jonathan alone about AIDS, when I hadn't?

"We all need to protect ourselves," I said. "They sell condoms in New Haven." I put the condom back on the nightstand. "Mom, you're trying too hard."

She looked at me fiercely. "I'm being polite."

"Jonathan doesn't want you to be polite. Polite is for strangers. You're his mother."

"They're not mutually exclusive, Ben."

She was right. But I wanted to tell her what I was thinking then, and what I've thought many times since. There's affection and there's propriety; there are things you do because you love someone and things you do to support a cause. My mother has worked harder to bring justice to the world than most people I know. But for her, Sandy isn't primarily my brother's boyfriend; he's someone whose rights she'd defend with her life. For my mother there's family and there's the rest of the world. You love your family; you stand on the picket line for the rest of the world. After all that Jenny and I have been through, my mother sometimes still treats her the way she would a diplomat, with a measure of deference that borders on the remote. My mother won't admit it, but she wishes we'd remain the boys we were, the babies she adopted more than thirty years ago.

Still, I thought, the seder had gone well. Everyone had gotten along with Sandy.

But later that night, after we'd done the dishes, Jonathan overheard my parents talking.

"Maybe it's genetic," my father had said. "Who knows for sure about these things?"

I realized what Jonathan thought—that my father had been saying that they'd made a mistake, that maybe they shouldn't have adopted him.

"Dad didn't mean it that way," I said.

"I'll always be a stranger to them."

"You're not a stranger to me. I'm adopted too."

"What does adoption have to do with it?"

"It's where we came from. It's what we share."

"I don't care where I came from. I could have come from the stork, for all the difference it makes."

"You don't mean that. You're just upset. Remember when we imagined we'd been flown to earth by spaceship? Don't you ever miss those times?"

"They were okay," he said, "but I've stopped dwelling on them. I don't know why you think about them so much."

We moved to San Francisco after graduating. I had no plans, so I went to California because Jonathan was going there with Sandy. I'd lived across the hall from him until we left for college, and across a courtyard all four years at Yale. He was the constant in my life, and I in his; I didn't see why anything should be different.

Also, I had a vague plan that we'd find our birth mothers. I never told him this. I didn't fully acknowledge it to myself. But the possibility was always there. We were living in the same city. Eventually we'd go on a search.

We arrived in San Francisco in September 1986. I held odd jobs for five years. I was a bike messenger, then a short-order cook at a taquería in the Mission district, then a proofreader for Stanford University Press, then a driver for the airport Supershuttle.

Eventually I got my teaching certificate at San Francisco State University. Since September 1992, I've taught American history to high school students in Berkeley at a progressive private school, where the students serve on the disciplinary board and call their teachers by their first names.

I'd always thought of myself as countercultural ("Countercultural?" Jenny once said. "Give me a break, Ben. Your father's a professor at Columbia. You grew up in an apartment on Riverside Drive. You went to Yale. You teach kids who will also go to Yale. Who do you think you're kidding?"), but when I arrived at the school, I realized that representing the counterculture wouldn't be my role. The principal wore blue jeans, and some of the male teachers had long hair. It was hard to tell who was a teacher and who was a student.

This made me uncomfortable. I believed in appropriate professional boundaries. I also thought students should learn the fundamentals. As "Ethics of the Fathers" says, five years old for Scripture; ten years old for Mishnah; thirteen for the Commandments; fifteen for the Talmud; eighteen for the marriage canopy. I've ignored some of the particulars, but I believe in the principle. A person should learn certain things at certain times.

So I made my students memorize names and dates. I had them recite passages from the Declaration of Independence, the Constitution, and the Gettysburg Address. I made them learn the names of all the presidents, vice-presidents, and secretaries of state.

My students, understandably, thought I was uptight.

"We love you, Ben," one of them said, "but you're a rigid guy in a suit."

"I don't wear a suit," I said. "I don't even own one." I took foolish pride in that.

"Are you married?" a student asked.

"Do you have a girlfriend?" asked another.

"This is American history," I said. "This is not the Phil Donahue show. If I ever get to be famous enough that my personal life becomes relevant to American history, then we can talk about my marital status."

Their first year in San Francisco, Jonathan and Sandy broke up. Jonathan went out with several other men. Again I worried about his health, but I knew better than to say anything to him.

Six months later, he and Sandy got back together. They've stayed with each other ever since. In the fall of 1987, Jonathan enrolled in UCSF Medical School. He has since completed his geriatrics residency. Medicine suits him well. The results are tangible and the pay is high. Sandy started Wiper-Up, a window-washing company. Now he employs three workers. He and Jonathan take vacations in the Bahamas and buy bottles of fine wine.

Meanwhile, my parents have aged. My father is fifteen years older than my mother. He was almost sixty-six when I graduated from college; he turned seventy-five this past year. He was always older than our friends' fathers. Perhaps that's why Jonathan chose geriatrics.

When Jonathan and I moved to San Francisco, we started going out to dinner together once a week. Several times each summer we watched the Giants play, sitting in the Candlestick bleachers eating nonkosher hot dogs. On Sunday afternoons when we were younger, we'd watched the Mets at Shea Stadium—my father sitting between us keeping score, my mother preparing us for summer camp, needle and thread across her lap, sewing name tapes on our underwear.

"Do you remember that?" I asked Jonathan once.

"Sure."

"Remember how we used to think Sandy Koufax was our birth father?"

But Jonathan wasn't interested in talking about adoption. It had been our shared language, but he'd moved on. I stopped raising the subject with him. I still thought about it—still thought that someday we'd go on a search—but I didn't talk about it with anyone.

Until I met Jenny. She wanted to know every detail about me.

We would stay up talking past five in the morning, when one of us would fall asleep midsentence. Jenny's rings and bracelets lay like scrap metal on the nightstand. Her earrings hung on hooks beside the vanity, swaying in front of the window. Sometimes she would leave her closet door open, and I would run my fingers along the pile of folded sweaters and the rows of pressed blouses. Pinned to the wall above our bed was a Venezuelan flag she had brought back from a trip to South America. Glass jars were spread around the room, holding Jenny's odds and ends: matchbooks from across the country, silk scarves, a rabbit's foot, a Tootsie Roll keychain.

An office was attached to the bedroom. On the cork board above the desk were old political buttons Jenny collected. "Henry Wallace for President." "54-40 or Fight." On the walls were photographs Jenny had taken of Tara and me. For a while Jenny thought about a career as a photographer. She still walks through the apartment with her camera around her neck, taking pictures. On the bookshelves were her casebooks and her legal manuals from the public defender's office.

My books were also on the shelves. We share the office; I live here too. But I travel light, Jenny says. I could fit all my possessions into a couple of suitcases. Why get attached to objects? I was happy to have Jenny decorate our home. It felt no less mine for her doing so.

Novels lay throughout the bedroom. Jenny loves Dostoyevsky, Tolstoy, and Chekhov; when she was a girl, she told me, she pretended she lived in nineteenth-century Russia. Sometimes at night we read aloud to each other before we go to sleep.

"Tell me what you were like as a child," she asked me once. "Make it so real I can see you."

On the floor sat a huge oak chessboard, made in England in the eighteenth century. It had been passed down through Jenny's family.

As a child, she had played chess with her parents; now she played with Tara.

I told Jenny stories about being adopted, how much it had meant to me as a child. I said that someday I might look for my birth mother.

"Why not look for her now?" Jenny said that if I knew where I came from I'd be able to get on with my life.

"Get on with my life? What makes you think I'm not getting on with my life?"

"You're a dreamer, Ben. It's like your life is out there in the future, but it's anyone's guess what that life is. Sometimes it's like you're watching yourself. It's as if you're not in your own body."

"I'm in my own body." I slapped the floor to show her I was there. I pounded my fists against my chest. "I'm here, Jen. Look at me. I'm in my own body."

"You should try being like Jonathan. He goes to work every day and comes home at night. He and Sandy make plans. They may be gay, but they live a more normal life than we do."

"We live a normal life. I go to work and come home every day. I don't know what you're talking about."

But I understood what she was saying. Though I'd moved into her apartment in January, almost two years after we'd started to go out, it hadn't been as simple as that. I moved in incrementally, shirt by shirt. One day I realized all my clothes were there and it made no sense to keep paying rent on my apartment.

In smaller ways too, I couldn't make a clear decision. I waited until the last minute to pay my bills. Once my phone line got disconnected. I didn't keep a date book, and I hated to make plans. Did I think I would die before the weekend came? Did I believe my birth mother would show up and everything else would become irrelevant?

"Live a life," Jenny said. "*Get* a life."

"I have a life."

"All right," she said. "All right." But she wondered whether maybe I should look for my birth mother, whether that might help me sort things out.

"It's possible," I said. "I'll think about it."

But I didn't think about it any more than usual.

"Things just take time." I ran my hand along Jenny's neck, down past the open buttons of her blouse, to the pale, freckled hollow between her breasts. "You don't plan a life. You grow into it. You only understand it when you're looking back. Besides, what's the point of making plans? Man plans and God laughs."

There I was, believing in my own way that everything was fine, that my life was moving ahead.

A month later the letter came, forwarded to me from my old address.

Dear Ben Suskind,

Almost thirty-one years ago I gave birth to you. I was sixteen and terrified, I was completely alone. Your father and I had no future together. I thought about keeping you. I *had* to keep you once I held you in my arms, and for the two months I had you I kept you by my side in a laundry basket in my bedroom. But I was a teenager and I had no money, and my parents insisted that we find a good home for you.

Thirty-one years is a long time. I know that. But I'm still your mother. I'm your flesh and blood. Not a week goes by when I don't think about you. Every year on your birthday I cry.

Eventually I got married to someone else. I moved to Indianapolis with my husband. But I've kept photographs of you from those two months we had together. I'm holding you in my parents' house, your hair's so soft and yellow, and my mother teaches me how to nurse you, while my father's on the phone, he's talking to agencies, he's placing ads in the paper, he's getting me to do what he says must be done.

I gave birth to a son nine years after you were born, but he got killed in a car accident last year (Scottie, my baby, rest his soul!), just before his twenty-first birthday. We haven't recovered, I don't think we ever will. Now more than ever I really need to meet you.

I'll be visiting California next month. I hope this isn't the wrong thing to say, but I feel like I love you (I *know* I love you, even if we haven't seen each other in more than thirty years), and I want to meet you when I come to visit.

Until then, you're in my heart and thoughts. With hopes for a happy reunion—

Your birth mother,
Susan Green

I didn't know what to do other than stand still. All my life I'd imagined this day, but now that it had come I couldn't feel anything.

Then I did something that surprised me, something I hadn't done in a long while. I went to synagogue. It was a Saturday morning, and I drove across the bay to Berkeley, to a synagogue I often passed on my way to work. Services were almost over by the time I got there, but I took a prayer book and joined the worshippers, although I didn't pray. I stared down at the words and listened.

Much has happened since then. But when I think about that day, what I recall beyond the letter is being back at synagogue, the familiar unfamiliarity, the rhythmic motion of prayer and the smell of kiddush wine, the rabbi's hand warm against my own as he wished me a good *shabbes*.

Jenny had made some phone calls on my behalf and gotten the name of a social worker who specialized in adoption; I could contact her for an appointment.

The social worker, who was in her mid-thirties, had grown up in Marin County, she told me when I met her. She had gone to good private schools and had parents who loved her, but until she found her birth mother she felt vaguely lost.

On the walls of her office were posters of eagles flying over the American prairie and of children of different races holding hands. Books lined the shelves—Shakespeare plays and some novels, a psychology text on parent and child. A few marbles rested on the floor. Next to the marbles stood a miniature yellow Mack truck.

"Mr. Suskind," she said, "what brings you here?"

I had come for Jenny, although Jenny would have denied that she cared whether I came or not. "You can just talk to her," Jenny had said, but what was there to talk about? I was going to meet my birth mother—I'd made up my mind.

I told the social worker the first lie that came to me. I said I wanted to adopt a baby.

"That's why you're here?"

"I think fatherhood would suit me."

"All right," she said, and she took out some brochures and outlined the possibilities. There were public and private adoptions; there were lawyer's fees. Some people, she said, had specific preferences. Did I care about gender? Was I willing to adopt a black baby? A Cambodian? A Vietnamese? "You're married, aren't you, Mr. Suskind?"

"No," I said.

"Then you want to adopt a baby on your own?"

"That's right."

"Are you gay?"

"No."

"How old are you, Mr. Suskind, if you don't mind my asking?"

"Thirty."

"Thirty. That's not very old. Have you considered waiting?"

"I've *considered* it."

"I don't mean to dissuade you, Mr. Suskind, but you're going to have some difficulty. You're an unmarried man. There are people's prejudices to contend with. Have you thought of other options? Maybe you could get a friend to help you out."

Jenny wasn't home when I returned from the social worker's, and I was immediately disappointed. She'd had a trial that afternoon; I'd forgotten that she would be late at work. I wanted her to be there so we could talk about what had happened, even though I understood that nothing really had happened. A week had passed since my birth mother's letter had arrived, and I'd been reduced to the infant she'd given up, needy and petulant.

These feelings surprised me. I don't mind being on my own. When I was twenty-three, I hiked the Appalachian Trail by myself. Occasionally I get into my car, drive up the coast, and spend time alone among the redwoods. But something had happened to me in the wake of getting that letter. I wasn't being myself.

I fixed dinner for Tara. She had turned eleven recently and had taken to eating only certain foods, although it was hard to determine which ones. She claimed to be a vegetarian, but once, at a

Chinese restaurant, she sneaked a piece of mu shu pork from Jenny's plate when she thought we weren't looking. For the past month, she'd been eating little else but Kraft macaroni and cheese. I don't like macaroni and cheese, but I made a big pot of it anyway.

"Where's Mom?"

"At work," I said. "She'll be home soon."

"She better. She promised to help me with math." Tara dipped her finger into the pot and dropped a gob of melted cheese into her mouth.

"I can help you with math."

She shook her head. "Mom knows fractions, and you don't."

I considered defending my knowledge of fractions, but thought better of it. "Well, she'll be here soon."

It was hard to predict how Tara would act, especially when the two of us were alone. She'd become more difficult since I'd moved in, although, when the move had become official, she'd been a big advocate of mine, decorating the apartment with Welcome signs. Several times before drifting off to sleep, she had murmured "I love you" in a state of semiconsciousness. She'd even told me that she preferred me to her father, although it was hard to know what that meant, since she saw him only once a year.

But she could be abrupt, turning sharp-tongued toward Jenny and me. She locked the door to her bedroom. Sometimes at dinner she placed a bandanna over her eyes, as if to say she didn't want to see us. She kept her CD player on loud late at night when she was supposed to be asleep, when Jenny and I thought she was asleep, Soul Asylum blasting through the apartment at eleven o'clock.

Still, I loved her. I'd courted her too when I'd first met Jenny, taking them to the circus and the San Francisco Exploratorium. I'd given Jenny white roses and bottles of French wine and bought comic books for Tara; I'd watched cartoons with her on Saturday mornings. On weekends, she and I had gone to museums, and to long animated movies in which hairy creatures beat each other over the head. As we sat at the back eating strands of red licorice, I worried about Tara the way a father would, all that violence, even in cartoons.

But I wasn't her father. Sometimes I wished he'd come and take her and leave me with Jenny for a while. I liked the time after Tara went to bed, when Jenny and I were too tired to speak, when we lay together in our room and listened quietly to music.

Now, though, Jenny wasn't home. I looked at the photographs she'd taken, some framed, some not, on our bedroom walls. In the morning I would come out of the shower and there she'd be, sitting on the floor in her bathrobe, taking photographs of me without my clothes on.

"Be careful," I told her once. "That's the kind of thing that will get you arrested. Drugstore clerks turn in photos to the FBI. Then you get charged with pornography."

"This is San Francisco," Jenny said. "That's why I moved here. No one cares what you do."

For her, San Francisco had been the answer to everything. She'd wanted to live here since she was a child, in the days when her family was zigzagging across the country and she dreamed that someday she'd have a real home. She liked the warm weather; she swore she'd never bring children up in a place where they needed a winter coat. As a teenager, she'd seen San Francisco on TV and been struck by the sheer beauty of it, but also by the people who were fighting for what was right. Even as a child, she'd had an exquisite sense of social justice. In Norman, Oklahoma, where she'd lived when she was twelve, she'd organized a food drive to help feed the hungry. In high school, in Billings, Montana, she volunteered after school at legal aid, licking and stamping envelopes. She moved to the Bay Area in the fall of 1980 to go to U.C. Berkeley. She met Steve there freshman year. They got married when they were juniors; the year after that, Tara was born. The next fall, separated from Steve, Jenny started Stanford Law School.

Now she was a public defender for the City and County of San Francisco. She spent her time defending habitual criminals—thieves, drug addicts, prostitutes, assault-and-batterers. Although most of her clients had done what they'd been charged with, Jenny had no qualms about defending them. There was some fun in beating the system, she admitted, but that was only a small part of it. Everyone was entitled to the best defense possible. Better that a hundred guilty people go free than that one innocent person be convicted. The legal process was what mattered. You fought for your clients as hard as you could, if only to raise some reasonable doubt, because your clients needed you and were entitled to your help. What chance did they have against the power of the state? Prison just made them worse, in any event. They came out a few years later more dangerous than before. And when you heard about their lives, your heart went out to them. In light of where they'd come from and what they'd endured, it would have been surprising had they not turned to crime. Jenny wouldn't have been any different; she was convinced of that. Besides, once you got to know them—once you got to know *anyone*, Jenny said—you couldn't look at them the same way. They might have committed a terrible crime, but they had a sense of humor, they were kind to their parents, they were capable of moments of grace. This was a cliché, she knew; Hitler, after all, loved kittens and little children; how many times had she heard that? But it was true. It was like reading a novel. You became involved in someone's life; you saw the person's humanity; you sympathized with human beings you wouldn't have expected to sympathize with.

Jenny was eloquent in defending her work. And one of the things she had liked about San Francisco was that for years her work hadn't needed defending. This was a liberal city, the ideal place to be a public defender. Jenny liked to run into her clients on buses and on BART; sometimes she would find them huddled on grates and would offer them a cup of coffee.

But times had changed. The former police chief was finishing his term as mayor; even in San Francisco people were hunkering down. There was a sense of fatigue and of indifference to the poor. Let the criminals fry, people said. California had a three-strikes law. At dinner parties and parent-teacher conferences, people asked Jenny what she did for a living, and when she told them, they looked rebuking and uncomfortable. People used to ask, "Do you like what you do?" Now they asked, "How can you do that?" A colleague of Jenny's was being stalked by a client the colleague had successfully defended, and when Jenny told this story to a couple of friends, they had little sympathy for her colleague. You reap what you sow, they said.

Even my brother gave Jenny a hard time. Jonathan, who at Yale had slept in a shanty, who at fifteen had campaigned for Barry Commoner for president, who once could recite the ratings given to every senator by Americans for Democratic Action: my brother had become law-and-order. Gays had been assaulted in the Castro; neighborhood groups had banded in self-defense.

"Would you defend absolutely anyone?" Jonathan asked Jenny once. "How about Hitler or Mussolini?"

"That's a silly question," she said. "Everyone uses Hitler as the absurd example."

"Would you defend someone who shot your mom?"

"That's even sillier." At law school, Jenny had learned that hard cases make for bad law. The same idea was true here. Some people were harder to defend than others. But it wasn't for her to decide.

I tended to agree with her. Although some of her clients were unsavory, I thought she was doing the right thing. Late at night in our bedroom I'd cup my hands over her small breasts, then place my ear to her sternum. "Jen," I'd say, "I can hear your heart bleeding."

She'd poke me gently in the forehead. "Don't patronize me."

"I'm not patronizing you." She did important work.

But late that night, when she finally came home, I wasn't feeling sympathetic toward the man whose case had kept her out late.

"Where were you?"

"At work," she said. "You knew that."

"Defending an ax murderer?"

"Drunk driving. What's gotten into you?"

"What's gotten into me is it's ten o'clock and you just came home. Tara had a fit because she thinks you're the only one who can do fractions. And I went to see a social worker because you wanted me to, and you know what we talked about?"

"You saw a social worker because *you* wanted to. It was your decision."

"Do you know what we talked about?"

"What?"

"Nothing." I paced around the bedroom in tight circles, then threw myself down on the bed.

"You're being a baby," Jenny said. "Cut it out."

I had waited to tell Jonathan about the letter. I didn't know how he would react. Now I handed it to him and watched him read it.

"Your birth mother?"

"So she claims." Suddenly it occurred to me I was going on her word. It could have been a hoax. She might have been mistaken. I could ask her to provide ID—a lock of my infant hair, a piece of information only she could know. I could require her to take a blood test.

"I have a feeling you're going to meet her," Jonathan said. He looked nervous, and that surprised me. I'd expected him to act indifferent, as he often does about family matters. Maybe the letter had awakened something in him. Maybe he was nervous because, although he wouldn't admit it, he too wanted to meet his birth mother.

"Do you want my advice?" he asked.

"Sure."

"Don't meet her."

"Why not?"

"Because you have a life to live. You've got a girlfriend to love and her daughter to help take care of. You've got students to teach."

"I'm not quitting my job or leaving Jenny. I'm just agreeing to meet this woman. We'll probably have coffee. It will be an hour out of my life."

"It will be a lot more than that. Trust me. It always is."

What did he know? Even if he was right, it was worth it, I told him, for me to find out about my past. It should have been worth it for him to find out about his also.

"Well, it isn't," Jonathan said. "I'm not interested."

"We used to talk about our birth mothers all the time. Don't tell me you weren't curious."

"I was, but I'm not any longer."

"You'll change your mind about this. Believe me."

I had no reason to think I was right. No reason other than the conviction itself, the belief that we were embarking on a joint venture.

I called my parents and told them about the letter. They talked to me through different receivers.

"Did you know about this?" I asked.

"That she was going to contact you?" said my mother.

"Right."

"We certainly didn't," my father said.

"What do you remember about her?"

"Please, Ben," my mother said, "it happened a long time ago. Does it really make a difference?"

"Of course it does."

"We were honest with you," my father said. "You always knew you were adopted."

"I know that."

"Whatever we remember," my mother said, "isn't likely to be true any longer."

"All right, then. Just tell me if I've got the right person. I don't want to go through with this if it's a mistake."

"Who wrote the letter?" my mother asked.

"Susan Green."

There was silence.

"Well?"

"Susan's the right name," said my father.

"But not Green?"

"Maybe she got married," he said.

My parents asked if they could get off the phone. They wanted to call me back a little later, once they'd had a chance to think.

Only ten minutes passed before the phone rang again. They asked me to come home for the weekend.

"*This* is my home," I said. "I live in San Francisco."

"We don't make very many requests of you," my father said. "I'd insist if I could." They needed to tell me something, he said, and it had to be in person.

My parents were standing at the gate when I got off the plane. They looked awkward—erect and attentive with their hands behind their backs, as if they were posing for a portrait.

I hugged them separately, then together. "Where's the cardboard sign?" I asked. Once, years before, they'd stood like chauffeurs at the airport gate, holding a sign with my name scribbled across it.

"We ran out of cardboard," my father said. He laughed, and my mother did too. But I could tell they were nervous; they stood uncomfortably before me in the glaring airport light and shifted their weight from one foot to the other.

During the car ride home, my parents told me several times that they loved me. I felt bad for them, my mother and father with their backs to me, repeating these words like a mantra.

"I love you too," I said.

"Still?" said my mother.

"Of course, still." Cars passed in the other direction, headlights flat and illuminated like sets of yellow eyes. The Manhattan skyline shone above the water.

"Will you call her 'Mom'?" my mother asked.

"No," I said. "You're my mother."

"She gave birth to you."

"You brought me up."

My mother leaned her head against the window.

"You can't change history," my father said.

"I'm not trying to," I told him.

We ate dinner by candlelight when we got home, my mother at one end of the table and my father at the other, sitting in an antique chair. He'd bought it at an auction many years before. It was delicate and expensive. When we were small, Jonathan and I hadn't been allowed to sit on it.

"I used to sit on that chair," I told him now.

"That's okay."

"Jonathan and I both did. We took turns on it while you two weren't watching."

"It was a long time ago," he said.

"We didn't mean any harm by it."

"It's just a chair." He hit the antique hard across the arm. "Just a bunch of pieces of wood."

"I think we made too many rules when you were small," my mother said. She patted her food with a spoon. "Ben, were you happy when you were young?"

"Sure."

"Are you happy now?"

"Most of the time."

"Because we want you to be happy," my father said. "That's the only thing we care about." His arms lay limp along the tablecloth; his hands were rough and hairy. Freshman year of college, I'd told him that I'd stopped being religious—that I didn't cover my head with a yarmulke and that I ate nonkosher food and that I went to football games on the sabbath. He had said nothing, but he'd looked palsied and liquid-eyed. I realized that he was getting older, that someday he was going to die.

"I remember when I first held you," my mother said. "It was the happiest day of my life."

"It was my happiest day too," said my father. When I was little I used to go into his study and watch him work; I liked just to be there while he marked his exams, while he penciled in tentative grades in Hebrew. I sat quietly beside him, and the way I imagined it, we were in something together, the two of us grading his students' papers. I would read through an exam and judge it by its handwriting, then ask him if I'd given it the proper score.

My mother rested her hand on my forearm. "Do you think Dad and I did all right by you?"

"Yes," I said.

"Because we did the best we could," my father said. He looked out the window, and my mother did too.

"You can meet your birth mother," my father said.

"Ben doesn't need our permission," said my mother.

"I know. But I want him to realize that he has it if he wants it."

The next day was Friday. I stayed home with my mother and helped her prepare for the sabbath. We roasted chicken breasts and made matzo balls for the soup. I laid the challah and the wine cups on the dining room table. After taking a shower, I put on navy slacks and a white oxford shirt. When my father came home, he smelled of library books and after-shave; he held out flowers for my mother. Standing in the living room next to the avocado plants, I watched my parents kiss.

After my mother lit the sabbath candles, my father blessed me. He rested his hands on my head and asked God to watch over me. As he did, I kept my eyes closed and my body erect. I tried to picture God, gray-bearded and munificent, protecting me from harm. I held my breath and just listened.

Later that night we sat in the living room. My father read the *TLS* and my mother read *The New Yorker*, and I lay on my back on the old sofa and listened to the sounds of the night. At midnight, the lights went off. The lamps were on timers—it was forbidden to turn them on and off during the sabbath—and we sat in the dark for a long time until my eyes adjusted.

"This isn't bad," my father said. His hand glided above him, taking in the darkness. "The sabbath. All these rules. You can't tell me it's a bad thing, Ben, this life."

I didn't say anything.

"It's what you grew up with," he said.

"Please," my mother whispered. "Leave Ben alone."

The next day I went to synagogue with my parents. I was called up to say the blessings on the Torah. I followed along as the reader chanted, as his fingers moved above the parchment. I felt the prayer shawl slung loosely over my shoulders, the tzitzis dangling by my waist.

In the afternoon we walked through Riverside Park, past the monkey bars where children played. "New crop of kids," my father said. He'd repeated that each spring when I was younger. But it touched me now in a way I hadn't remembered. I thought of all the rituals that wove through our lives, the shalts and shalt nots and the phrases we repeated, the way we told ourselves that nothing much had changed.

Above us the oak trees swayed. We passed through triangles of refracted light. "I had a dream the other night," my mother said, "and the strange thing is, I wasn't even in it. It felt as if I were watching my own life."

"I've felt that," I said.

"Ben," she said, "where are you going?"

"Now? I'm walking with the two of you in Riverside Park."

"I mean in general. What path are you taking?"

"Please, Mom, don't ask me these questions."

"Will you meet your birth mother?" my father asked. The veins in his forehead shone through the skin like tiny blue tracks.

"Yes," I told him.

"We could come along when you meet her," my mother said.

"Please, Mom." I wished she wouldn't talk this way. I wished this didn't upset her.

"We'd be respectful. We'd be there to offer you moral support."

The shadows extended before us, blotches of evening on the speckled concrete. In less than an hour it would be dark. My father would recite the *havdala* service. We'd drink the wine and smell the spices; then a new week would begin. The next day I'd return to San Francisco. Already I could feel my parents' unhappiness. I worried they thought that I'd never come home again, that things wouldn't be the same between us.

"Do you remember when you were a teenager," my mother asked, "and you wouldn't let Dad and me hold your hand?"

I nodded.

"It was just for a while."

"I'm sorry," I said.

"It's okay. That's how teenagers are." She looked at me sadly. For an instant I felt something strong between us, something basic and ineffable, almost in the blood.

"I remember when you were small," my father said. He stared up at the sky as if he were peering through a telescope, as if my former self were suspended there like a planet. "I've never told you this before, but there were times I'd wake up in the middle of the night and I'd go down the hall to check on you boys. I was afraid something had happened to you."

"We were afraid a lot," my mother said.

"One time," said my father, "I saw a U-Haul parked outside the building, and for an instant I thought someone had come to take you." He turned to face me. "You need to know something." He glanced at my mother, then back at me. "You weren't born Jewish." He stood before me, awkward and penitent. He looked as rigid as a marionette.

"What do you mean?"

"Jewish babies weren't easy to find," my mother said.

"Next to impossible," said my father.

"So we converted you," my mother said.

My father nodded. "The rabbi dunked you in the *mikve*. The mohel performed the bris."

My mother shuddered. "It's barbaric."

"It's a commandment," said my father.

"You lied to me," I said.

"You're Jewish," my father said. "That's what's most important."

"You could have told me."

"A Jew is a Jew," my father said. "A Jew is a Jew is a Jew."

I couldn't fall asleep that night. My parents had lied to me. Now it seemed so obvious I felt foolish for not having realized it before. All my life, I'd thought my birth father's name was Abraham. That was what my parents had told me. It was how I'd been called to the Torah, Benjamin the son of Abraham. I used to flip through the pages of the Manhattan phone book looking for men whose first name was Abraham. I wrote down their addresses and phone numbers, and kept the list in my desk drawer.

But my birth father's name wasn't Abraham. That was how converts were called to the Torah. They were all sons of Abraham. Abraham, our forefather, the founder of Judaism. He'd broken his father's idols; he was the first Jew.

Jonathan was called to the Torah as the son of David. But maybe my parents had lied to him as well, only this time they'd constructed a more elaborate story, actually providing a made-up name. If Jonathan found his birth mother, we might learn we were related by blood: two Christian babies abandoned on the subway, as in a headline from the *New York Post*. Then the story I'd told him about *The Guinness Book of World Records* wouldn't have been a lie after all.

I might have been able to pass for a Jew. I didn't have a pug nose or ruddy Irish cheeks; my hair had grown a bit darker over the years. But I didn't look especially Jewish. My features were straight, and my neck was thick, like the necks of the football players I'd known at Yale. After basketball practice in high school, my teammates had joked about how I looked. "Hey, Jesus, pass the soap," they said. I laughed with them and pretended not to notice. Had I simply not wanted to recognize the truth?

Halfheartedly I considered searching for my birth mother back then. I asked my parents who she was. They said they'd tell me when I turned eighteen.

On my eighteenth birthday, my parents threw me a surprise party. They invited my friends from school and summer camp, everyone I knew in a huge bowling alley. Rock music played on the speakers. The drinking age was still eighteen. Standing by the flickering pinball machines, my father bought me a can of Schaefer beer. Schaefer. The beer that sponsored the New York Mets. As I popped open the tab I looked at my father, who was also drinking a Schaefer, my father who didn't like beer, who never before and never since drank a beer with his son.

I understood even then what my parents were doing. They were hoping to drown me in the party, to make the day pass without my noticing that I could find out who my birth mother was.

I said nothing about this. Not that day or the next. As the days passed and then the weeks, I wondered why knowing was important to me. I had parents who loved me. Couldn't I control my curiosity when I realized how much this upset them?

"I'm not Jewish," I told Jenny when I returned to San Francisco.

"What are you talking about?"

I described what had happened in New York.

"But your parents converted you, so what difference does it make?"

Yes, my parents had converted me, so technically I may have been Jewish. Even that I wasn't sure of. But I couldn't look at myself the same way.

"Why not?"

"Because if your mother's Jewish, then you are too. And if she's not, you're not."

"But your mother *is* Jewish."

"Not my birth mother. She's the one who counts."

It was no longer clear what made me Jewish. Had I been Jewish only because I thought I'd been born Jewish, and now that I was wrong, I wasn't a Jew? If my parents hadn't converted me and everything else had stayed the same—the sabbath, the kosher home, the Jewish day school—I wouldn't be a Jew no matter what I thought. I couldn't be counted for a minyan at synagogue. Now that I'd stopped being religious, my parents' revelation worried me even more. I was living with someone who wasn't Jewish. I had nothing to fall back on.

"Let's say someone's mother is Jewish," Jenny said, "which makes that person's mother's mother also Jewish. How far does it go back, anyway?"

"To Abraham."

"You think every Jew is descended from Abraham?"

I was inclined to say yes. But that sounded about as reliable as claiming that the world was five thousand years old.

"Fine," she said, "then you're not Jewish. It makes things easier for both of us."

"If only it were so simple."

It bothered Jenny the way my parents behaved, always kind and polite when they saw her, but also always distant. Even my mother, who, under other circumstances, would have loved Jenny (they had a lot in common, I thought), could be curiously remote around her. My mother herself wasn't religious; she'd simply compromised for my father's sake. I was surprised that it was important to her that I marry a Jew. But it *was* important to her. She quietly allied herself with my father, who thought my relationship with Jenny would someday end, who still phoned me with the names of single Jewish girls, with the silent breathless weight of his hoping.

I thought of turning to a rabbi. But I didn't know any rabbis. Before I'd gotten my birth mother's letter, the only times I went to synagogue were when I returned to New York. The day her letter came, however, I chatted with the rabbi after services in Berkeley. He struck me as a decent man. When I called him now, he agreed to meet with me.

Rabbi Stone's office was in the back of the synagogue. The air smelled familiar, the sweet fermented scent of Manhattan's Lower East Side, where my father grew up and where our teachers took us to see matzo made by hand and the sabbath wine bottled.

Rabbi Stone told me a little about himself. He had grown up in New York City, in an assimilated Jewish home on Central Park West. He'd gone to the Trinity School, where the students attended chapel every morning despite the fact that many of them were Jewish. His parents had had a Christmas tree, although they'd called it a bush and decorated its branches with Stars of David. Jesus was Jewish, his parents had said. They liked to remind him of that.

When he got to Princeton, Rabbi Stone found God. He studied at a yeshiva in Israel and came back to the United States to prepare for the rabbinate.

He was more or less my age. Several times since I'd met him, I'd seen him on the streets of Berkeley carrying a knapsack on his shoulder, not looking like my idea of an Orthodox rabbi. He had no beard. His head was always covered, but sometimes he didn't wear a yarmulke—instead sporting a Brooklyn Dodgers baseball cap with the peak turned slightly to the side. I'd watched him from afar at Berkeley Bowl, strolling through the produce aisles with his infant son in a front pack.

He asked me now about my religious education. I'd told him that I'd gone to Jewish day school. He wanted to know if I'd studied Talmud and if my Hebrew was fluent.

I'd learned Talmud, I said. I could still speak Hebrew and make my way through the prayer service. The day I'd met him, I'd been surprised by how familiar the liturgy sounded. My grade-school teacher, Rabbi Appelfeld, had described Jewish learning as a car without brakes: either you were going forward or you were going backward. But there I'd been in synagogue that morning, and all the tunes came back to me.

"You wanted to talk about adoption," Rabbi Stone said.

I nodded. "But first I need you to promise not to judge me."

"Why would I judge you?"

"Because you're an Orthodox rabbi. You think a Jew's supposed to live a particular way, and by those standards I don't do very well."

He looked kindly at me. His eyes were gray, the color of quartz; they sparkled briefly in the synagogue light. "I have my beliefs. But I only preach to those who want to be preached to. Besides, that's not what you've come to talk about."

He opened a volume of the Talmud and read to me. "*Kol ha'migadel yatom b'toch bayto, ma'aleh alav ha'katuv ki'eelu yilado. Kol ha'milamed ben chavayro Torah, ma'aleh alav ha'katuv ki'eelu yilado.*" He translated: "Whosoever rears an orphan in his own house is considered by Scripture as if he fathered the child. Whosoever teaches Torah to the son of his companion, Scripture considers him as if he begat him." King Saul's daughter Michal reared the children of her sister Merav and therefore was considered their mother. Even Batia, the daughter of Pharaoh, was deemed Moses' mother for having saved and reared him.

For most purposes, Rabbi Stone said, my adoptive parents were my parents from the perspective of Jewish law. When they died, I should say kaddish for them. I was obligated to obey them, as the Torah commanded.

Still, he said, adopted children were like orphans. They should be treated sensitively.

"I'm not an orphan," I said.

"Not literally."

"Not figuratively either." Behind him, on a bookshelf, the volumes of the Talmud were lined up. Next to them were the Five Books of Moses. Squeezed on other shelves were scores of commentaries in Hebrew and Aramaic. Some I'd heard of, some I hadn't; some were almost a thousand years old. It was depressing how much there was and how little I knew. I, who in many ways was an educated Jew, had turned my back on this tradition without fully learning it.

"I have two parents who love me," I said.

"Of course you do."

"But you consider me an orphan."

"Not exactly." He opened his desk drawer and removed a sheet of paper. It was a bibliography he'd prepared for me. I felt bad for having been rude to him. He didn't even know me. It wasn't clear what I'd done to deserve his kindness.

"I didn't mean to be impatient."

"Jews are an impatient people."

"But I wasn't born Jewish." I felt as though I were sitting before a great arbiter of law, before God himself. I hoped that Rabbi Stone would release me, that he'd recast my life with his long rabbinic fingers and tell me I wasn't Jewish.

"You're a Jew," he said. "If your conversion was valid, as I gather it was, if you were raised a Jew, as you say you were, if you continued to practice even after your bar mitzvah, then you're a Jew according to the law."

I felt great disappointment and great relief.

He spoke to me in Hebrew: "*Yehoodee hoo yehoodee af al pee she'yechetah*. Do you know what that means?"

I did, I told him. I'd heard those words from Rabbi Appelfeld. *A Jew is a Jew even if he sins*. It was impossible, Rabbi Appelfeld had said, to convert from Judaism.

My father's words came back to me. A Jew is a Jew is a Jew. I was a Jew, but I wasn't. I didn't care what Rabbi Stone said. I didn't, and I did.

I got up from my chair and shook his hand. I thanked him for meeting with me.

As I reached the synagogue doors, he called out. "Come back anytime."

"To synagogue?"

He was standing in the shadows at the front. The light from the ark shone on his head, casting him in swaths of orange. "Why not?"

"I don't believe in God. It would be hypocritical for me to go to services."

"You came once."

"That's true."

"And you've been before. The door's always open."

"Thank you. I don't expect to come back, but I appreciate your offer."

Three weeks to the day after her letter arrived, my birth mother called. She was flying to San Francisco the following afternoon and wanted to meet me the day after that for lunch.

Perhaps she, like my parents, would spring news upon me. You've inherited a terrible disease. You've been bequeathed ten million dollars. I saw myself at lunch with her, still numb, thinking: *You're thirty years old, and you're meeting your birth mother for the first time. What are you feeling right now?*

I didn't feel anything.

Two days later, I waited for her at an Ethiopian restaurant on Telegraph Avenue in Berkeley. I loved Ethiopian food, this restaurant especially. I wanted to show her my good taste. This is my town, this is my restaurant, as if I myself had cooked the food.

But now I wasn't sure I'd made the right choice. She lived in Indiana. Perhaps a hamburger would have been better. Briefly, on the phone, I'd asked her what she looked like so that I wouldn't embarrass myself in the restaurant, moving from patron to patron, asking every woman whether she was related to me. But my birth mother hadn't been specific. She looked average, she said. I'd seen a magazine cover with a picture of the "Average American" on it. It was a computer composite of various races, weights, and body types. Maybe that was my birth mother, a goulash of strange people come to find me.

She'd asked on the phone if I would pick her up at the airport, but I'd refused. I would see her, I said, though not at an airport, a place constructed for reunions. Maybe she would try to hug me. I didn't want her to, and I didn't want her not to.

At work the day before, I'd kept glancing at my watch, waiting for the time her plane would arrive. While lecturing on Jim Crow, I tossed my chalk from hand to hand; I found myself looking out the window. She seemed to be everywhere now that she'd arrived. I almost expected her to land outside school and get off the plane and greet me.

I thought of her as a homeless woman, pushing a shopping cart off the airplane, showing up at the apartment with her bric-a-brac. In the morning I'd wake up and find her stuff on our floor—magazines, chewing gum, old packets of tissues. She'd comb through our fridge for leftover food, leaving cellophane wrappers crumpled on the counter.

A woman walked toward me in the restaurant. The black leather pocketbook slung over her shoulder thumped against her side. "Ben," she said, and stuck out her hand. "Susan Green." She was smaller than I'd imagined, almost a foot shorter than I was. She had a wide symmetrical face, while mine was longer and narrower, and pale green eyes, while mine were blue. Her skin was darker than mine, but we both had sandy hair. Her nose was straight like my nose; her nostrils were evenly parted. But what I noticed most was how young she seemed. She looked like a Catholic schoolgirl.

"Hello, Mrs. Green." She wore a navy blazer and a gray wool skirt; around her neck was a string of pearls. In each earlobe was a tiny gold stud in the shape of a star; I smelled perfume on her. Her hands were small but muscular. I was struck by the strength of her grip, and by the ease with which she held herself. I'd been expecting someone more retiring.

"You recognized me," I said.

And she said, not unkindly, "Mother's intuition."

She looked around the restaurant. I'd been right to second-guess myself. She seemed unsure about the place, glancing up and down the aisles. Then I saw what was bothering her. The patrons were eating on the floor.

"We can sit on chairs if you want."

She seemed slightly embarrassed. "It's Ethiopian food, right?"

"Don't you like it?"

"I've never had it." She reached into her pocketbook and took out a tissue, then rubbed it gently across her lips as though she were worried there was something there. She checked the pockets of her blazer to make sure the flaps weren't stuck inside. "They don't use utensils here, do they?"

"Do you want to go somewhere else?"

She hesitated. "We don't really know each other."

"That's true."

"Maybe next week."

"Maybe next week what?"

"Maybe next week we can eat here."

"Next week?"

"Or the week after."

How long was she staying in town? Part of me hoped that she planned to stay forever, that she was uprooting her life for me. But if she told me that, I'd panic and bolt. It would be like a first date. You had just met, and the girl was already saying that she wanted you to meet her parents.

"There's a Chinese place across the street," I told her.

Before I could say anything else, she was out the door and crossing Telegraph Avenue, weaving through the traffic.

But when we reached the Chinese restaurant, she changed her mind. The place was too dark, and the menu had pictures of all the items. "It's like Denny's," she said. "It's the first time we've met, and I don't want to feel like we're eating at a Denny's."

We walked up the street toward campus. We passed salad bars, taquerías, sandwich shops, and pizza joints. We stopped in front of the restaurants and glanced at the menus, but at each place something else seemed slightly wrong. We were dancing around each other: You choose; no, *you* choose. We really must have looked as if we were on a first date, all elbows and knees as we walked up the street, unable to find the right distance between us, several times almost colliding with each other.

Finally we settled on a combination restaurant and music store across the street from campus. We sat on the landing, where the menu offered sandwiches, quiche, and fresh-squeezed juices. On the floor below us compact discs were for sale. Classical music came from the speakers.

"Do you feel comfortable here?" my birth mother asked.

"I'm fine," I said. In truth I was nervous.

She closed her eyes. She was concentrating on the music, a plaintive strain of cello and violin. "Do you like classical music?"

"It's okay. My parents played it all the time when I was a kid, but I never really was interested in it."

"I like classical music." She paused for a few seconds. "What do you like?"

"In general?" I tried to think of a good example, but I couldn't come up with anything. I was uncomfortable with the conversation. It felt like an interview, my birth mother asking me lots of questions, trying too hard to learn who I was. "What do *you* like?"

"I like the beach," she said. "I like a good meal. I like Italian food. I like getting the chance to meet you, Ben. That's what I like most right now."

"I'm glad to meet you too," I said.

"You don't have to be polite."

"I'm not being polite. I really am glad to meet you."

She smiled at me, then took a sip of water. "I like to read. I like to open a good novel before I go to bed."

"What do you read?"

She thought for a while. "Danielle Steel and Rosamunde Pilcher.

I like the kind of book you can take to the beach." She smiled tentatively, as if seeking my approval. "I like James Michener too."

Danielle Steel. Rosamunde Pilcher. James Michener. I also love to read, I always have; on the way home from school, I often stop at the public library. I make sure to read at least a novel a week. I wished my birth mother had mentioned an author who surprised me—André Gide, Paul Bowles, even someone as popular as Jane Austen—anything to suggest we had more in common than I thought.

"I like Marcel Proust," I said. Proust was a great writer, but I hadn't read that much of him. Was I simply trying to contrast myself with her, to make her tastes seem philistine?

"What else do you do?"

"I play basketball," I said. I wasn't sure why I'd brought this up. Basketball was fine. I'd played in high school, and at Yale I'd spent a season on the junior varsity bench, getting beaten up under the boards during practice. I still played pick-up twice a week, but basketball wasn't my life. It wasn't the best way to describe myself.

"Your birth father played basketball."

"He did?"

"I used to watch him on the playground after school."

His image came to me, this man whom for years I'd thought of as Abraham. Every Abe I'd met, every Abraham: I'd examined him as if for a mark, wondering whether he was related to me.

"Did you love him?" I asked.

Her eyes grew moist. "Very much."

"Didn't he love you?"

"For a while he did. For a while we both loved each other."

"But then?"

She looked sadly at me. "Then we got older."

What, I wondered, had gone wrong between them? If I'd been their son—if I'd *stayed* their son—maybe I'd have been able to patch things up.

We went to the counter to get our food and then returned to our table. My birth mother raised her sandwich to her mouth. "I want to know everything about you," she said. "I want us to catch up."

That was what I wanted too. So why did I feel compelled to tell her the truth? "We can't catch up."

"Why not?"

"Because I'm thirty years old. We can sit here and talk. We can be cordial to each other."

"But I want us to be more than cordial." She reached her hand across the table. For a second I thought she was going to touch me. For a second I wanted her to.

"You've never been part of my life," I said.

"I know that." She looked downcast. She had her hand on her water glass. Her fingers made slender imprints in the condensation.

I could have told her that I loved her and that I didn't. Why had she brought me into this world? Why had she left me, and why had she waited? Why, right now, had she finally come back, this woman who was sixteen years older than I was, who sat before me after all her troubles and looked young enough to be my sister?

"Mrs. Green—"

"Please, Ben. Susan."

"Susan."

"Tell me what you're thinking."

"I'm not thinking anything right now."

"Then tell me the first thing that comes to your mind."

So I told her that, when we were children, Jonathan would take a picture of me every month. "I used to line up the pictures," I said. "I was trying to figure out the person I was becoming. I wanted to pinpoint the moment I changed."

"I like the person you've become."

"But you don't know me."

"I want to *get* to know you."

I wanted to get to know her also. But what if she tried to take over my life? What would Jenny think—Jenny who had encouraged me to meet her but who hoped that, in doing so, I'd move on? I had no idea how you got to know someone when you were trying so hard to do just that. You could fail from all the effort.

Perhaps I'd grow bored with her. Or maybe she'd grow bored with me. If we'd met under different circumstances, we might not have had anything to talk about. What could be worse than being bored by your own birth mother?

"How did you find me?" I finally asked.

"I tracked you down."

"Right, but how?"

She cupped her hand in front of her face as though she were about to tell me a secret. But I knew no one in the restaurant besides her.

"I hired a private detective," she said.

"To follow me?"

"To find out where you were."

"Susan." Had someone been following me to and from school? Had this person been peeping through the windows? I was angry with Susan, although at the same time I was touched that she'd tried so hard to find me.

"It was the only way to contact you," she said. "For a while when you were small I was living in New Jersey, and I used to take the bus across the George Washington Bridge and come down to Riverside Park and watch you. But then I moved to Indiana."

"You used to watch me?"

"I was always careful. No one knew who I was."

I used to see strangers in Riverside Park, idle men and women sitting on the benches, feeding bread crumbs to the pigeons. One of those strangers might have been Susan. My parents had warned me not to talk to strangers. I'd heeded their warnings with such diligence and fear that even when I was asked what time it was I looked down at the pavement and kept walking. Children could be kidnapped, just like Patty Hearst. Had Susan thought of kidnapping me? I'd read about birth parents who changed their minds and tried to retrieve their children.

"Is the detective still following me?"

"He found you," she said. "I don't need him anymore." She stared down at her lap. "I'm sorry."

She sounded sincere. I didn't know what to do other than to tell her I forgave her.

"A week ago," I said, "I found out you weren't Jewish."

"You thought I was?"

"It's what my parents told me. I believed it all my life."

"Your parents don't approve of me, do they?" She'd left a tiny slice of turkey on her plate, pale and milky as a sliver of moon.

"Why would they disapprove of you? You're the person who brought me into the world."

"That's true." She seemed happy to hear me say this.

She told me that her ancestors had come from Scotland, and I in turn told her about my Jewish heritage.

"I stopped being religious in college," I said. "But when I was a kid, I thought I'd be a baseball player in the spring and summer, and a rabbi the rest of the year."

Then I told her about Jonathan, Jenny, and Tara.

"I know about them," she said.

"What do you mean?"

"You already mentioned your brother."

"And Jenny and Tara?"

She seemed to regret having brought this up.

"Your detective?"

She nodded.

"Susan—"

"I'm sorry. But I would like to meet them."

I wanted her to meet them too, but I wasn't pleased that she already knew about them. I considered laying down some ground rules. We'd meet only so often and in certain locations; we'd meet on my terms or we wouldn't meet at all. But I couldn't get myself to do this. I kept thinking of myself reversing our roles, treating Susan as if she were my child: This much TV, be home by midnight, don't dye your hair green, no beer in the house.

"Why did you track me down?" I asked.

"It seemed time. When your child dies, it gets you thinking."

"I'm sorry." I'd forgotten that her son had died. I wanted to tell her I'd do all right by her; I'd try not to let her down.

"There are articles about this. When a child dies, the sort of strain it puts on a marriage."

Was she talking about her own marriage?

"Another reason I've flown here is that I make earrings, and some stores in San Francisco want to sell my work."

"Is something wrong with your marriage?" I asked.

"My husband and I are on a trial separation." She looked embarrassed. "I'm not good at much, am I?"

"Of course you are."

"Like what?"

"You just told me about your earrings. You live in Indiana, and stores in San Francisco want to sell your work. You must be good at that."

"But important things."

"That's an important thing."

"Is your work important to you?"

"Sure it is." I told her I was a schoolteacher.

She seemed about to say she knew this as well.

"What happened after I was born?" I asked.

"I was sad for a long time. I was in eleventh grade when I got pregnant with you, and when I started to show I dropped out of school. You almost had to then. Times were different."

"And afterward? Did you go back?"

"I got my GED. I'd always planned to graduate from college, but things didn't work out that way. I spent a year in junior college and a year in secretarial school. Then I met my husband, and we moved to Indiana for his work. He's a manager at a bank, and he got me a job there. I've been able to save some money."

She got up, as if she'd seen someone she knew. But then her gaze dropped and she simply stood still. She began to search through her pocketbook. "Ben, I want to have a picture of us." She removed a Polaroid camera from her pocketbook.

My school was on the other side of town. That was why I'd met Susan on Telegraph Avenue—so I wouldn't run into anyone I knew. I'm a private person, but it was more than that. It was as if I didn't want there to be a record; I could pretend that this lunch hadn't taken place. No one cared about our reunion. Our pictures wouldn't show up in the *National Enquirer.* Still, I worried. Meeting my birth mother and not meeting her. This was the story of my life. One foot in and one foot out, never able to commit myself.

But before I had a chance to object, Susan had approached the man at the next table and asked him to take our picture. We stood behind my seat; Susan had her arm around me. Aside from our handshake, this was the first time we'd touched.

"Smile," the man said. He pressed the shutter button, and the photograph shot out. He pressed the button again.

We watched the photographs develop. Susan handed me one and kept the other. I felt tears in my eyes. Seeing that picture of Susan and me, I was overcome by grief for everything I'd lost, for all that hadn't happened between us.

I turned away from her and wiped my face.

When I turned back, she was staring at the photo. "Ben." Her voice had grown softer. A line of mascara dripped down her cheek. "Do you think we look alike?"

"The two of us? We have the same color hair." I grabbed a lock of mine as if to demonstrate, as if I were speaking a foreign language.

"Other than that, I don't think we do." All my life, I'd imagined that I looked like other people, that I had siblings and parents, carbon copies of myself somewhere on this earth, if only I could find them. I simply didn't think I looked like Susan. I would have told her if I did.

"Well, *I* think we do. What about genetics? Don't you ever wonder how much in life is determined?"

"In college I wrote a paper about the paradox of free will."

"I'm not talking about that. We share the same blood."

"I know."

"Half your genes come from me."

"Thank you."

"Thank me what?"

"Thank you for giving them to me."

I wanted more than anything to be patient with her, to treat her without malice or irony. But I wasn't responding well to her pressure. I wished I lived thousands of years ago, a man in a loincloth roaming the fields who did nothing more complicated than pray for rain.

"They've done these studies of identical twins," she said. "The babies are separated at birth and raised in different homes, but they grow up to be extremely similar. One twin goes to the bathroom and flushes the toilet twice. The other twin lives hundreds of miles away, but when he goes to the bathroom he does the same."

"So what?"

"Two flushes. Tell me that's a coincidence." Her blouse hung open at her neck; freckles dotted her skin, brown and dense. "I gave birth to you. You can't change that."

"I'm not trying to." I didn't know what she wanted from me. To acknowledge that without her I wouldn't be alive?

She rested her hands on the table. Her knee brushed against mine. I flinched.

"Will you tell me about my birth father?" I asked.

"He was my high school boyfriend. I haven't seen him in more than thirty years."

"What's his name?"

"What difference does it make?"

We were quiet now. We had run out of things to say. How was that possible? We had whole lives to reconstruct. But an hour had passed, and already I didn't know what else to talk about.

Susan got up and walked to the register. She stood at the door, a shimmering figure in the early-afternoon light.

When she came back, she was holding a rose. "For you," she said. She stuck out her hand. The flower's head was pink and bent; its petals were hunched like someone in prayer.

Hesitantly, I reached out to take it. "Thank you."

For a moment she stood there gripping the stem, her fingers firmly wrapped around mine. For a moment I let her hold my hand.

We stood outside the restaurant, watching students walk past. We didn't know what to do. It *had* been a date. In a way it felt like a one-night stand. Inside, it had been as though no one else were with us; the other patrons had receded. But now, amid the cars and the wave of bookbags, we saw each other in the harsh light. There was a world staring back at us. Perhaps that was why we didn't make plans to see each other again. Maybe we just panicked.

I reached out to shake Susan's hand. "It was good to meet you."

"It was good to meet you too."

We walked in opposite directions. When I turned around a few seconds later, I wasn't able to find her.

There were so many questions I'd forgotten to ask her. How much longer would she be here? Was she staying at a hotel, or had she rented an apartment? I hadn't even gotten her phone number. She'd offered to go out for Ethiopian food the next week, so the odds were good that I'd see her again. But I couldn't be sure. I wanted to continue a relationship like this, Susan wishing to spend time with me and me resisting, all the while hoping she'd continue to call.

I was exhausted when I got home. "I'm drained," I told Jenny. "It feels as if I did a thousand push-ups."

"What was she like?"

"She was a lot of different things." But I couldn't come up with even one way to describe her. The whole lunch was a haze; I had no idea who she was.

I showed Jenny the photograph of us.

She gasped.

"What?"

"She looks so young."

"She's only sixteen years older than I am. When my mother was her age I was still in high school."

"She's pretty," Jenny said.

"You think so?"

"Very."

I supposed she was. It hadn't occurred to me to think of her as pretty or not pretty. She had component parts: green eyes, wide face, dark skin, straight nose; she was this, and I was that. But the whole of her, the full image, escaped me even now as I stared at her photograph.

"Do you think I look like her?"

"Not really," Jenny said. "You're pretty too, but you look different."

I was disappointed to hear Jenny say this. I'd been hoping she'd see something I hadn't noticed.

"Did you like her?" she asked.

"Mostly it felt like she was real. That's the hardest thing—giving up your fantasies. I used to think my birth mother was an Arabian princess and a brilliant researcher at the NIH. Not one or the other, but both."

"Ben—what was she like?"

"She was a little pushy, I guess. But I couldn't have expected her to be calm."

I tried to sum up the meal for Jenny, yet everything I said felt inadequate.

"How long will she be here?"

"I don't know. I was meaning to ask her, but I forgot. I'm starting to think this is just the beginning."

"Of what?"

"I thought this would be like opening a curtain—I'd see what was behind it, and that would be that. But you open the curtain, and there's another one behind it. And another and another."

Jenny said nothing.

"Susan makes earrings," I said. "That's part of the reason she's here. Because of me, of course, but also because some stores in San Francisco want to sell her work."

"She's an artist?"

I nodded. "I'm embarrassed to say this, but it made a difference to me. It made her seem more substantial."

I wrote my parents, wanting to tell them what had happened, as if failing to do so would be a betrayal. I tried to assume a breezy tone—both casual and reassuring.

Dear Mom and Dad,

I had lunch with my birth mother today. We had a nice time. She doesn't look like me—at least I don't think so. Do you think I look like you? They say that when you live with someone long enough you begin to resemble them. Some people even start to look like their pets. I'm glad things weren't reversed—that I wasn't raised by Susan and meeting you two for the first time. Think of all the catching up we'd have to do.

The weather's warm here. That's one of the nice things about California. I've almost forgotten what snow looks like. Remember the story you once told me, Mom? How the first time you saw snow you thought it was sugar piled on the cars?

Teaching is going pretty well. My students think I ask them to memorize too much, but Jonathan tells me they'll be grateful for this someday. Short-term memory goes first, he says, but his patients recall a lot from their childhoods. So I can be confident that, sixty years from now, my students will be able to recite the Gettysburg Address. Remember what we learned in "Ethics of the Fathers," Dad? How when a child learns, it's like ink written on new paper, but when an old person learns, it's like ink written on paper that's been erased?

Jenny's doing well. She continues to keep long hours, working hard to defend people in trouble. I think you both would be proud of her. Whoever said that our generation is selfish—that we have no interest in politics and just sit around watching MTV—hasn't met Jenny. I hope you'll get to know her better and recognize what I see in her.

Tara is good too. We get along most of the time, although she thinks I know nothing about fractions.

I love you, Mom and Dad. I hope you're doing well.

Love,
Ben

I went to Jonathan's house to tell him I hadn't been born Jewish. I'd waited long enough. My news would come across as something serious, something I'd contemplated for a while.

But he didn't seem interested or surprised.

"Did you know?" I asked.

"I suspected it. What were the chances your father's real name was Abraham?"

"There are lots of Jewish Abrahams."

"Like who?"

"Abe Beame, for one." We used to pretend that Abe Beame was my father. Mayor Beame, who'd brought New York City to the brink of bankruptcy. We'd been in sixth grade when that had happened.

In the next Democratic primary for mayor, we handed out leaflets for Mario Cuomo before he lost in the run-off to Ed Koch.

"If it's any consolation," Jonathan said, "I'll give you my Jewish birth. It's more important to you."

"How do you even know you were born Jewish?"

"Because my birth father's name is David."

"Mom and Dad might have made it up."

"Whatever. Either they did or they didn't. It doesn't make a difference to me."

I didn't know how he could say that.

I told him I'd met my birth mother that day. I did my best to describe what had happened, but again the words seemed inadequate.

"Tell me something," he said. "Do you think she had the right to come looking for you?"

The right? What did this have to do with rights? He was adopted too; he should have understood. We weren't dealing with abstractions. "Of course she did."

"Our mothers gave us up at birth, Ben. I can't blame them. I don't know what the circumstances were. But a person has to live with the consequences of her decision. You can't go bursting into someone's life."

"What about us? If we made the first move and searched for our birth mothers, would we have the right to find them?"

"We might have the right, but it wouldn't be smart. Besides, have you thought about Mom and Dad? You know how much this is going to upset them. Don't you think we owe them something?"

In a fit of anger I almost said, "What about you? Do you owe them so much that you should live straight? Do you owe them a daughter-in-law and grandchildren? Don't lecture me about disappointing Mom and Dad."

Jonathan leaned toward me. "Let's say my birth mother knew when she got pregnant that, if she gave me up, I'd find her someday.

It might have been too much for her to bear. Maybe she'd have had an abortion."

Of course this had occurred to him. It had occurred to me too. When you're adopted, everything's contingent. All roads are mired with offshoots; you always see the path not taken. No wonder I studied philosophy in college, all those counterfactuals piled on each other. What if? What if? What if?

A letter arrived, written by my mother and signed by both my parents.

Dear Ben,

We got your letter. We were happy you had the chance to meet Susan. (Do you call her that directly? Susan? Mrs. Green? It must be hard to figure out the etiquette.)

The weather's good here too, though you're right, it's not as nice as where you guys live. Dad thinks if we lived in California we'd miss the change of seasons. But I'm sure we'd get used to it. We'd probably have more trouble with the pace. No one seems to work very hard out there.

Life's been busy for both of us. Things are tougher than ever for the homeless. Mayor Giuliani is the worst. I see those advertisements on the subways—the ones with the thought bubbles coming from a passenger upset that a panhandler is invading his "space"—and I just want to scream. Have you ever noticed how many homeless people panhandle with pets? It's a sad state of affairs when people are more willing to help dogs than human beings.

I'm glad you're proud of the work Jenny does. Dad and I are too. It's true that we don't know her very well, but the little I know of her makes me think that she must be decent and principled. I've never imagined her as someone who watches MTV all day long. You or Jonathan either. If the world had more people like you boys, we'd be doing a lot better than we are.

Send our love to Jonathan. We hope you're well. We'll talk to you both soon.

Love,
Mom and Dad

I was rereading the letter when they called. Telepathy, perhaps. I was prepared for them to sound as casual as their letter, but they seemed concerned.

"What was she like?" my father asked.

"She was friendly," I said. I didn't want to be more specific.

"Come on," my mother said.

I was blocked, my brain rattling with adjectives, as if I were writing a personal ad for Susan.

My father must have read my mind. "What if you had to write an essay about her? How would you describe her to your readers?"

Always the teacher, my father. Compare and contrast your birth and adoptive parents. Describe your birth mother in five hundred words or less.

"Are there particular things she likes to do?" my mother asked.

"She likes to read."

"That's good," said my father.

"Why's that good?"

"Come on, Ben. You're a big reader yourself."

Already I could see why I was resisting. My parents were sitting in judgment. It's good that she reads; it would be bad if she didn't. I too had been a snob. I disapproved of Susan's choice of authors; I was happy she made earrings. But my parents were judging me as well. Is our son's birth mother intelligent? Does she have good taste?

"Does she work?" my mother asked.

"She makes earrings."

"But how does she support herself?"

"That's part of the reason she's come to San Francisco. Some stores want to sell her stuff."

"She'd have to be unusual," my mother said, "to make a living off her jewelry."

"Maybe she *is* unusual."

"Of course she is." Several seconds passed in silence. I knew my mother was worried that she sounded condescending. She *was* being condescending, but she was also serious. "She gave birth to you, Ben. She's the most special person in the world."

"Please, Mom."

"It's true."

"Does she have views?" my father asked.

"Views?"

"You know. About the world."

"Everyone has views, Dad. She's a human being."

"But what are they? Does she have opinions about politics or religion, for example?"

Was he checking whom Susan voted for, this woman who came from the state of Indiana, home of the great Dan Quayle? As for religion, I was tempted to remind him that *he*'d had ideas about her religion. He'd told me she was Jewish.

"I only spent an hour with her. How can you expect me to answer that?"

I knew the question we were heading toward. It came next, from my mother.

"Did she go to college?"

My parents must have suspected that she hadn't gone to college. She'd given birth to me in high school. I could have told them that she'd done some junior college, but that would have confirmed their prejudices. Were they trying to remind me that they were better educated than she was? Education, attainment. My father had gotten his Ph.D. from Harvard and was one of the most respected scholars in his field. My mother had gone to Vassar and then briefly to Yale Law School and now was a professional success. She'd become an expert on the homeless; she was quoted in *The New York Times*. They'd been proud of Jonathan and me when we'd gotten into Yale, but to them it had been a matter of course. Was there any doubt that we'd go to the best colleges? Then Jonathan enrolled in medical school, while I floundered around for several years before getting my teaching certificate. Teaching was important. My parents knew that. When Jonathan and I had been in high school my father had served on the advisory board, urging the school to raise salaries so that better teachers could be hired. He too was a teacher. But he was an academic. That made all the difference. He never said this directly (he couldn't have; he wouldn't have), but he was disappointed that I'd become a high school teacher; I'd set my sights too low. He frequently asked me about my plans. His attitude toward my teaching was like his attitude toward Jenny: This is all right for now, but what comes next?

"What difference does it make if she went to college?"

"It doesn't make a difference," my mother said. "We just want to know about her."

"But it's *what* you ask about. Are education and career the only things that matter? Why don't you ask me what music she likes or what her favorite movies are?"

"Okay, what music does she like?"

"She likes the Sex Pistols, Mom. She screams like hell when Sid Vicious comes on the radio. She shoots heroin into her veins, and she's got a big tattoo on her butt. All right?"

"Ben," she said coolly, "we just want to make sure you don't end up disappointed. You've gotten all worked up about her, and you don't even know if you'll see her again."

"I'll see her again."

"Have you heard from her?"

"No."

"Well? She could have gone back to Indiana and not even told you about it. People like her are notoriously unreliable."

"People like her?"

"She gave you up. She doesn't have a particularly good track record."

"Jesus, Mom. She was sixteen years old. You should try to be a little more gracious."

"We don't mean to be ungracious," she said, "but you're our son. Your interests are what we're most concerned about."

I couldn't continue this conversation. I had to get off the phone.

But once I did, I couldn't stop thinking about what my mother had said. Was it possible that Susan had gone back to Indiana? It had been two weeks since our lunch, and I hadn't heard from her.

In a mild panic, I tried to track her down. I opened the yellow pages and called hotels in the city. I called motels, youth hostels, and bed-and-breakfasts. I spent two hours searching, but without success.

Exhausted and angry, I dialed information, in case she wasn't staying at a hotel and had decided to list her number. There were no Susan Greens but several S. Greens, all of whose numbers I took down.

I called the first number and heard Susan's voice when the phone was picked up. I was too shocked and relieved to say anything.

"Who's this?" she asked.

"Susan?"

"Ben."

"You recognized my voice."

"Of course I did."

I felt the seeds of anger. "You had my number. You could have called me."

"I was waiting for you to call *me*. You could have looked me up." She had made the first move, she said, by flying to San Francisco.

Now it was my turn to show some initiative. "This relationship is a two-way street."

"Don't kid yourself, Susan. You're the one who started this. You put me up for adoption, and then, out of the blue, you show up again. You incur some obligations, you know."

"I realize that. I just didn't want to smother you."

"Why are you in San Francisco, anyway? For me, I assume."

"That's part of it. And to sell my earrings."

"Does that mean you're here indefinitely?" Now I was worried she'd never leave. She'd buy property in San Francisco. She'd purchase a house next door to Jenny and me.

"I told you. My life is in flux. Nothing's definite right now."

"Well, you're living somewhere, aren't you? I assume I haven't reached you at a pay phone."

"I've rented an apartment in the Mission. I have a month-to-month lease."

When I got off the phone, I helped Jenny take the laundry out of the dryer.

"Susan's living in the Mission," I said. "She's renting an apartment and playing mind games with me. 'You call.' 'No, *you* call.' Who knows what she's doing with her time?"

"I'm sure she's occupying herself."

"But doing what?"

I thought of a joke I'd heard as a child. What's ambivalence? It's when your mother-in-law drives your new car off a cliff. Now ambivalence was this: When your birth mother moved to town, and you worried she would call you and wouldn't call you, and mostly you found yourself waiting for her, anxious about her, breathless as a ghost, waiting to see what would happen.

PART II

Childhood: When Jonathan and I had been so close we'd half believed we were each other. The year we were nine, we switched identities once a month; we swapped bedrooms at night and went to school in each other's clothes.

"My name is Jonathan," I told my mother.

"I like your name just the way it is."

But on the day we switched identities, I refused to answer to any other name.

"If I had to be someone else I'd be you," I told Jonathan.

"And I'd be you," he said.

In my father's closet was a tattered fur hat that he no longer used; he let Jonathan and me cut it into pieces. Jonathan covered his arms with the fur, the way Jacob had done to trick Isaac, dressing up as Esau.

Jonathan quoted from the Torah. "The voice is the voice of Jacob," he said, "but the hands are the hands of Esau."

We went to a nursery school sponsored by the Cathedral of St. John the Divine, because our Jewish day school didn't start until kindergarten. Before Christmas break, the teacher announced that Santa Claus was coming to school. There was a moment of silence, and then Jonathan's voice:

"Who's Santa Claus?"

"Don't you know anything?" I asked.

Embarrassed by his ignorance, he took it upon himself to learn about Santa Claus. The following year, outside Gimbels, he sat on Santa's lap.

"Jews don't sit on Santa Claus's lap," I said.

"I do." He told me he was going to convert to Christianity.

But in second grade, without explanation, he decided that Christianity made no sense. I found him in his bedroom making fun of Jesus, pressed to the door as if he'd been crucified.

We'd learned at Jewish day school that some branches of Christianity were considered idol worship. You weren't allowed inside a church—even, the Talmud said, if your life depended on it, even if you were fleeing from a murderer.

Riverside Church was up the block from our home. It was a huge building; we had once picked it out looking down from an airplane. When Jonathan and I practiced tennis against its wall, I thought of my father years before, playing handball on Delancey Street.

"Why can't you go inside a church?" my mother asked.

"Because it's idol worship," I said.

"That's nonsense." She'd visited churches all over the world. She'd stood in Notre-Dame; there was no feeling, she said, like looking up at the ceiling of one of the most beautiful buildings in the world. Late at night, I found her sitting with my father in the living room listening to Handel's *Messiah*. "If I had my way," she said, "I'd take you boys to churches, mosques, and ashrams. It's important to see how other people live."

But she didn't have her way. Jonathan and I went only to synagogues. And we continued to hit tennis balls off Riverside Church. It was a beautiful building, my parents said, but we knew what went on inside it.

"They eat Jesus' body," Jonathan said, "and wash it down with his blood."

"No they don't," said my mother.

Jonathan and I didn't believe her. Jonathan pressed his back against the wall of the church, pretending to be crucified. "We're idol worshippers," he said. He stood frozen like that against the building while I hit the tennis ball again and again, seeing how close I could get to his body without actually hitting it.

When we were ten we searched for our birth certificates. I knew I was born in July 1964 and Jonathan was born that December. But we couldn't find our birth certificates. We didn't believe we had real ones.

"You have birth certificates," my mother said.

"Were we born in a hospital?" I asked.

"Of course you were."

"I was born," Jonathan said, "by the banks of the Nile." He liked the story of Moses' birth, this baby left in a bassinet in the water, taken by Pharaoh's daughter to be brought up by the king.

My mother smiled at Jonathan. "You were born in a hospital like everyone else."

She wouldn't be more specific than that. We wanted to know how much we'd weighed at birth. We wanted to see our birth certificates.

"I don't know where they are," she said. Her eyes had the glossy cast of someone beginning to forget. I told her she was growing senile.

"I'm not growing senile. I'm being normal. Normal people sometimes forget."

I didn't believe she'd forgotten about our birth certificates. We had slipped into the world without anyone's noticing; there was no real record of us.

My mother had read us a book called *Are You My Mother?* in which a bird goes from one animal to another, asking whether she has given birth to him. Jonathan and I did the same thing. I had always been careful not to talk to strangers, but now I made an exception. We went up to women walking along Broadway and asked, "Are you my mother?"

At home we made our own birth certificates and laid them before us.

"Mom and Dad burned our real ones," I said.

"They used them as kindling," said Jonathan.

For years we watched the Knicks on TV. Our favorite player was Bill Bradley, who had gone to Princeton, where my father once lectured. Bill Bradley had a photographic memory; he'd been a Rhodes scholar. We thought that with practice we could be like him, so we came home from school and sat on our beds, trying to memorize the phone book.

"Forget it," Jonathan said the year we turned eleven. "We'll never be as smart as Bill Bradley."

In school we'd learned about the rabbis of old who could put a pin through a book of the Talmud and name every letter the pin passed through. Jonathan told me Bill Bradley could do that.

"Bill Bradley doesn't even know what the Talmud is," I said.

"Yes he does."

For Jonathan's eleventh birthday, I bought him *Twenty-one Days to a Better Vocabulary*. We worked on our memories, testing each other on words we didn't know. We took the phone we had made from two cups and string, and whispered to each other through it.

"Hello," I said. "Hello, my brother."

"Eulogy." He tugged on the cord to make sure I was holding on.

"Encomium."

"Panegyric."

That spring, he enrolled in a speed-reading course. When he came home from class he pretended he could read as fast as he turned pages, and I pretended I believed him.

"I read *The Book of Lists*," he said. He flipped through hundreds of pages, then pressed the book against his forehead to show me how much knowledge he'd absorbed. "I'm reading through every book in the library. Soon there will be nothing left to know."

We played on the basketball team and sang in school chorus. We took almost all our classes together. In seventh grade, we decided to study Spanish instead of French, though we knew our father would be disappointed. He'd been stationed in France during World War II and believed every cultured person should study French.

"French," he told us, "is a beautiful language." We were sitting in his study. On the shelf behind him were the books he'd written: *War and Empire in Soviet Russia. Leninism: A Life and an Idea. Doing the Dance: Soviet Jews and the KGB. A Francophile Visits Russia.* He'd dedicated this last book to Jonathan and me.

"It's a language for frogs," Jonathan said. We wanted to learn Spanish so we could communicate with the Puerto Rican kids in Riverside Park. We played basketball with them after school, shouting "*¿Qué pasa?*" as we ran down the court, as though we could speak Spanish too.

"It's a language of great literature," my father said. He and my mother spoke French to each other when they wanted to tell secrets. Jonathan and I listened carefully, hoping that if we concentrated we'd start to understand.

But most of the time we pretended not to care.

"I hate French," Jonathan said.

I, though, wasn't sure I did. Our parents had met in France. The way I thought of it, if it weren't for France everything would have been different. Jonathan and I wouldn't have been born.

"Of course we would have," Jonathan said. "We just would have been adopted by someone else."

"Like who?"

"Rich people. They can never give birth."

The only French person I liked was Jean-Baptiste de Lamarck, whom I'd learned about in science class. Lamarck believed that acquired traits were passed on from one generation to the next. I planned to acquire my father's traits and pass them on to my son.

I sat at my father's desk, wearing his glasses, studying the books before me. I examined him at dinner, trying to make the faces he made. When dinner was over, I stood in front of the mirror and stared at myself. My plan was working.

"I'm starting to look like Dad," I told Jonathan.

"No you're not."

"I've taught myself Yiddish," I lied. "I know everything about political science."

I used to worry about my parents' fifteen-year age difference, thinking that was the problem: my father had been too old to have children, so my parents had to adopt.

"Mom and Dad never had sex," Jonathan said.

"Yes they did." I was nine. I understood these things.

"Have you ever seen them?"

I hadn't, I admitted. I'd never even seen them naked.

We'd learned in school about declining sperm counts, all those cells like worms our teacher chalked across the board. But once, in the supermarket checkout line, I read about a ninety-five-year-old who had fathered sextuplets and whose wife was pregnant again.

"A ninety-five-year-old can't father sextuplets," my mother said. "You're lucky at ninety-five to even be alive."

"It happened," I said.

"Then we'd have heard about it. It would have been in *The New York Times*."

"It happened in Brazil."

At night I lay in bed and worried about my father. I was sure he was the reason my mother couldn't give birth. I told her what I thought.

"He wasn't the reason."

"Then who was?"

"No one. Sometimes things happen for no reason at all."

But nothing just happened. Maybe my father had done something wrong. What if I couldn't have children?

It was possible my wife hadn't been born yet. If I was fifteen years older, she wasn't even a cell under a microscope.

"My wife doesn't exist," I told my father.

"There's no way of knowing that," he said.

He taught Jonathan and me that every person has a *bashert,* his missing half, the person God chooses for him to marry. In class we learned about atoms and subatoms. Our science teacher liked to explode things; she stood before us in a long white coat. Her face was white too, covered with chalk dust. She drew atoms on the blackboard, huge ovals like flying saucers, particles colliding in the electron field.

That was how I saw the world, millions of people circling one another. It was coincidence whom you met and whom you didn't. I thought about what my father had said, how we each had a *bashert,* how God had His plan.

I didn't yet like girls, didn't want to have a girlfriend, but still I wondered about my *bashert.* At dinner my father would quiz us on geography. He'd ask us the capitals of all fifty states. He'd have us locate Timbuktu on an unmarked map. On the wall above my desk hung a huge map of China. What would I do if my *bashert* lived in China? I saw my *bashert* and me without a word in common, forced to wed by God's command.

"It's not a command," my mother said.

"Then what is it?"

"Think of it as a prediction. God is simply placing a bet."

Still, I believed I had a *bashert.* Every morning, I said a prayer that she be someone I loved, someone I could spend a life with. I was compassionate, my mother said. I gave money to the beggars on

Broadway. There was a boy in my class who had cerebral palsy; during recess, I pushed him in his wheelchair while my friends played dodgeball in the gym.

I was doing a mitzvah, my father said. God would reward me in the world to come.

But I was concerned about this world. Rabbi Appelfeld had told us that God tests people with inner strength. I hoped I didn't have inner strength. I imagined myself with a wife like that boy, someone to wheel about and feel sorry for.

Jonathan and I said we'd travel the world, but mostly we wanted to be like our father, who'd traveled the world in uniform, fighting the Germans in World War II. He was a professor of political science; he never went to work without a jacket and a tie. But years before, he'd been someone else. He'd spent a thousand nights inside army barracks. He went for weeks with little food or sleep, keeping himself sane by reciting poetry. He helped the other soldiers compose letters to their girlfriends, mud-stained declarations of love and honor, carefully honed sentences in fountain pen. He was a poet himself, his army mates thought.

Unarmed, he'd come upon a battalion of Germans. His German was rusty, but he managed to communicate, getting the Germans to lay down their weapons.

"How did you do that?" I asked him once.

"Persuasion," he said. "It was 1944, and the war was almost over. It was clear we were going to win. I told the Germans the Senegalese were coming. The Senegalese were rumored not to take prisoners."

"*Were* the Senegalese coming?"

"It was possible. I wasn't sure."

I liked hearing him tell stories about the war, liked holding the objects he'd captured. He had a pair of German field binoculars so powerful that when we used them at Shea Stadium we could see the color of the batters' eyes. He had a gray wool blanket with German writing across it. Sometimes at night, lying beneath that blanket, I tried to picture him when he was young.

Was this why I feared I would die, knowing my father could have been killed in World War II and everything that followed would have been different?

Was it simply that I was adopted?

I imagined that my birth mother had died. I persuaded Jonathan that his birth mother had died too. "They died in childbirth," I said.

"How do you know?"

"Telepathy. I have ESP."

In school we'd learned about our foremother Rachel, who for years had been unable to bear a child and who was buried by the roadside on the way to Bethlehem after giving birth to Benjamin. "Benjamin killed Rachel," I said.

"No he didn't."

"We killed our birth mothers too."

I thought about this on Yom Kippur, the year I was ten, crying out to God and hoping not to die. In synagogue we read a list of ways to die—plague, famine, pestilence, fire—deaths too awful even to think about. A family down the block from us had been killed in a fire, so every week that year when the sabbath was over I held the *havdala* candle lit beneath the smoke alarm to make sure the battery was still working.

"You're being silly," my mother said.

"I'm protecting the family." I stood on a stool, holding the candle high above me, and when the alarm began to blare, I told Jonathan that we were safe for another week, that God would protect us until the next sabbath.

"God doesn't protect us," my mother said. "The smoke alarm does."

"You don't know anything," I told her.

I kept my door open when I went to sleep at night, hoping to hear the smoke alarm. I'd be like my father in World War II, guarding the battalion from death and Hitler, reciting poetry.

"I hate poetry," Jonathan said after school one day.

"Poetry kept Dad sane during the war."

"So what?"

"So it's important." I thought about this when I went to bed that night. Lying beneath the blanket my father had captured, I couldn't fall asleep. I didn't want to fight in a war; I lacked my father's courage.

"I don't want to die," I told Jonathan the next day. "I don't want to get flown back in a body bag."

"They've got nuclear weapons now. If you die in a war, you'll get blown to pieces. There won't be a body to fly back."

I imagined my parents during World War II. What was my mother thinking while my father was in combat? How could she have known the danger he faced, this girl who wasn't yet a teenager, who lay in bed at night listening to the radio for news from the battlefront, who saved her allowance to buy provisions for the soldiers? Maybe those provisions reached my father. I saw him crouched in his foxhole, eating a can of beans my mother had sent him, grateful for her kindness.

For a while I thought he'd been injured in the war—and that was why my parents couldn't have children.

"Maybe Dad got his balls blown off," I told Jonathan.

"He didn't get his balls blown off."

"Maybe he has some kind of disease." I read about diseases I'd never heard of, and convinced myself I had them. "I have Lou Gehrig's disease."

"No you don't," Jonathan said. "Only Lou Gehrig had that disease. That's why they named it after him."

"Lots of people have Lou Gehrig's disease. Thousands of people in the United States."

People with Lou Gehrig's disease had trouble swallowing, so in fifth grade I started eating my food without chewing it, in the hope that with practice I could improve my swallowing.

"You're a healthy boy," my mother said. "People with Lou Gehrig's disease are much older than you."

I didn't believe her. I read about rare neurological conditions, about bacteria-carrying insects, and viruses that existed only in the jungle. And I continued to eat without chewing.

"You'll choke," Jonathan said. "That's what you'll die of—asphyxiation."

He wasn't worried about disease, but he was happy to pretend he wasn't well, if only so we could be a team.

"I have whooping cough," I said. I stood before my mother and whooped as I coughed.

"I have the mumps," said Jonathan.

We knew about the mumps from *The Columbia Medical Encyclopedia*. People who had the mumps sometimes lost their hearing, so Jonathan pretended he was deaf. "I have to go to special mumps school," he said.

"I have cervical cancer," I said. Then I felt bad, because my grandmother had died of cervical cancer; now she was in heaven, looking down at us.

"Only girls get cervical cancer," Jonathan said.

For months after that he pretended I was a girl. "You have breast cancer," he said.

"No I don't."

"You need to go to a gynecologist."

Mostly we pretended we were sick so my parents would let us stay home from school. They rarely believed us, though. As a boy, my father had once had a subnormal fever; he placed the thermometer on top of the radiator so that it would look as though his temperature had risen and he could go to school. Colds went away, he reminded us. Mind over matter.

In Riverside Park he played baseball with us, and explained the physics of a swing and how a pitcher could achieve maximum velocity.

"Step into the ball," he said. "Think about physics."

But I wasn't interested in physics. I was interested in playing for the New York Mets. In the park, as the sun began to set and the pigeons fluttered above us while my father hit us grounders, I could smell beer and peanuts. I pretended I was Tommie Agee and my father, in left field, was Cleon Jones. My mother waved to us from the balcony of our apartment. She looked like a fan in the bleachers. I pictured the whole neighborhood out on the balconies, everyone's mother rooting me on.

Over dinner, sweaty and spent, my father taught us how to chant from the Torah. That was our deal. He played baseball with us, and in return we agreed to learn the notes. My father's brother Marvin, who lived in Chicago, was the best Torah chanter my father had ever heard. He was the champion Torah chanter of the Windy City.

"There are no champion Torah chanters," Jonathan said.

"He's my champion," said my father.

We had potential, he said. We had good voices and good minds; with a little practice we'd chant as well as Uncle Marvin.

"Who cares?" said Jonathan.

"I do," I said. Now I felt bad, because Jonathan and I were supposed to be in this together. But I did care. I wanted to be like Tommie Agee. I'd be the first Jewish center fielder the Mets had ever had, the only player who could chant from the Torah. I'd be older but the same, gazing up at the planes as they dipped toward La Guardia, and at the stands where my parents would be cheering.

I thought of my father growing up on the Lower East Side, where he'd played stickball on the streets. His family had come from White Russia, eleven consecutive generations of Eastern European rabbis. As a child, he'd walked from kosher butcher to kosher butcher along Essex Street, past shops that sold mezuzahs and tefillin. At home he spoke Yiddish, on the streets English. On Passover, he said, you couldn't find bread—not a crumb in any store. He had a fantasy in which the president of the United States was Jewish and all the hot dogs at Yankee Stadium were strictly kosher.

This was my fantasy: I'd be the starting center fielder on the New York Mets, and at the peak of my career I'd boycott Shea Stadium. I'd boycott every stadium in major-league baseball until they all sold kosher hot dogs.

Then I thought of Roberto Clemente, who had died in a plane crash on a charity mission. What was the point of keeping kosher if God could let that happen? Was this the moment that I started to doubt God?

In ninth grade, Jonathan and I discovered girls. We each had a girlfriend, and sometimes the four of us went bowling together or stopped at Carvel to eat ice cream and play pinball, breaking up into teams.

"We could play couple against couple," Jonathan said.

"Or brothers against nonbrothers," I suggested.

Sometimes after school I went to the movies with my girlfriend. As the images flashed across the screen I dropped Raisinets into her open mouth and let her lick my fingers. I took her to *The Deer Hunter,* and when the scary scenes came on I rested my hand against her thigh until, gently but firmly, she removed it.

One time Jonathan met me when the movie was over. He had spent the afternoon at his girlfriend's apartment listening to Bruce Springsteen. Jonathan liked the line from "Born to Run"—"Strap your hands across my engines"—but he and his girlfriend had to leave the door open whenever they were in her bedroom alone.

"Can you believe it?"

"No," I said.

"Springsteen never had rules like that."

We knew the words to all of Springsteen's songs. We cut out articles about him. He was from New Jersey, where everyone had sex. We couldn't imagine he had any rules at all, or that he even had parents.

For months and months we listened to him. We played his music until the vinyl got scratched and his voice grew even raspier than it actually was. We sat in the living room listening to him, staring across the Hudson at New Jersey.

"We'll swim there," I said.

Jonathan agreed.

We pressed our noses against the window. Our breath came back to us, frosty against the glass, in the puckered-up shape of our mouths. Across the river were refineries. Behind them, we imagined, New Jersey girls were waiting, saving themselves for the two of us.

At work, things were changing. There, especially, I found myself thinking about Susan. I'd lecture about family life in colonial America, and I'd think, I too have a family. I saw myself in everyone and everyone in me.

I began to feel great tenderness for children. Not only adopted ones, but children of all kinds. I smiled at children on the streets, expecting them to see me as a kindred soul, a male Mary Poppins. When I overheard them arguing with their parents, I instinctively assumed they were right. Adults were impatient, I thought. I failed to recognize that I was an adult and often impatient with Tara.

I sentimentalized my students and exaggerated my importance in their lives. Sixteen and seventeen years old, juniors in high school, they seemed fragile to me, as if they were toddlers and I was their parent, when in fact they were on the cusp of adulthood, many of them sexually active, the girls full-figured, the boys starting to sprout mustaches, several of them as tall as I was and able to compete with me on the basketball court.

At the same time, I was having a crisis of confidence. What good, I wondered, was American history? Even if it did some good, how much would my students remember in a year? Would they even remember me? I knew that feeling of running into an ex-student and watching him or her grope for my name. I'd forgotten many of my own teachers.

I was cramming my students with facts. But I wasn't sure any longer what purpose these facts served. I knew a lot of facts myself. Evenings, I played along with *Jeopardy!* and got most of the answers right, but this didn't do me any good. I wasn't any less confused than before. I read a novel a week; I actually kept a list of the books I'd read. But even if I lived to be eighty-five, I would read fewer than three thousand more books. That wasn't much when you considered what was out there. What would I have to show for myself?

I wanted to make a difference in my students' lives. I can hear myself saying this, almost coaching myself—"Ben, you need to make a difference in their lives"—a notion so self-serious it makes me cringe, but I felt it quite strongly. In my mind, my status had been raised: history teacher, guru, personal savior. Years from now, my students would come back and tell me I'd changed their lives. But how? By teaching them about the Monroe Doctrine?

So I tried to turn my classes into something new. In one section of American history, I strayed from the syllabus and became confessional with the students. I stopped class early one afternoon and told them that history needed to be grounded in the present, that we'd been treating old laws simply as old laws and that these laws were embedded in a context.

I spoke about slavery as it related to genealogy; I talked about European feudalism, primogeniture, and the divine right of kings.

"This is American history," one student said. "There are no kings in America."

"That's true," I answered. "But if we knew how the colonists felt about kings, specifically about King George of England, we'd understand a lot about American history. We'd understand the separation of powers and the struggle for the Bill of Rights. We'd know why the Articles of Confederation were ratified and why they lasted only a few years."

I instituted a section on oral history, because, I told my students, history wouldn't make sense unless we personalized it. They would talk about their lives and relate them to their studies. I assigned memoirs and personal correspondence. I told my students to read *The Diary of Anne Frank*.

"Anne Frank was Dutch," a student said. "Why are we learning about her in this class?"

"American and European histories are intimately related," I answered. In college, I told my students, interdisciplinary studies were the rage. "Boundaries are breaking down. Everything is being cross-referenced."

"So what?" said the student. "This isn't college. Why can't we just be in high school for now?"

"Be patient. I promise you'll enjoy this experiment."

At the end of the week, I told my students I had an announcement. "Something important has happened to me. I'm adopted, and recently, for the first time, I met my birth mother."

The students looked uncomfortable. What had happened to the rigid guy in a suit, who made them memorize every secretary of state, not to mention every president and vice-president, who refused to say whether he was married or had a girlfriend, because it had nothing to do with American history?

"Ben's being weird," one student said. "He's having an identity crisis."

"I'm not having an identity crisis."

But was I? I had a student named Paul who'd been adopted as an infant; his mother, concerned about his work at school, had told me this. Paul had never been one of my favorites. He was intelligent, but his grades were mediocre. He sat in class and looked out the window. Sometimes he composed limericks on the back of the school newspaper. His sole ambition, he told me once, was to play guitar with Courtney Love. Between classes, I would find him sitting in the student lounge, staring straight ahead, with his shoes off.

Now, however, I started to take a greater interest in him. He was the reason I'd chosen this class for my experiment. Sometimes after school I'd sit next to him while he played his guitar, doing my best to sing along. He was adopted, and so was I. Aside from Jonathan, I'd never had an adopted friend. I would do my best to befriend Paul. I wanted him to know that I understood him.

May came, and with it the flowers in the rose gardens in Berkeley and along the bike paths of Golden Gate Park. The stores were filled with lilies and tulips, nature conspiring to remind everyone that Mother's Day was soon.

"This feels like a crucible," I told Jenny.

I'd seen Susan once more, and things hadn't gone especially well. She'd had an extra ticket to a sneak preview of *Apollo 13* and had asked me to come along.

I sat with her in the theater for two and a half hours, offering her popcorn and sips of my soda. I felt the shock of electricity as I brushed against her sweater and quickly pulled away.

She liked the movie, and I didn't.

"It's because you're too young," she said. "If you were older, you'd understand what the country was going through at the time. Everyone was scared. Nobody turned off their televisions."

"I wouldn't have liked the movie any better even if I was older than you. I don't like suspense movies. And I'm not interested in movies about space. I never even saw *Star Wars*."

"What about Tom Hanks? Didn't you see *Philadelphia?*"

I had. But I knew we weren't going to agree. We had different taste in movies.

"Well?"

"Yes, I know. Everyone loved *Philadelphia*."

"Did you?"

"I thought it was a little manipulative."

"Manipulative? Maybe you didn't like it because the people in it were gay."

"Susan," I said, "my brother's gay."

"He is?"

Hadn't I told her? I was tempted to say that her private detective had been loafing on the job. She appeared to be reevaluating everything about me. But she said nothing more about Jonathan's being gay—not then, and not after.

"I went with Jonathan and his boyfriend," I said, "and none of us especially liked it."

Already I could see that nothing would be simple between us. Everything would take on greater meaning. I liked this movie, and you didn't. Are we really compatible? Are we meant to be together? I didn't want to fight with her. I've gone to many movies I didn't expect to like. It isn't a huge concession.

"If you don't like suspense movies or movies about space, why did you come along?"

"Because you invited me."

"I could have gone with someone else."

"Okay, do you want me to spell it out? It didn't matter to me what the movie was. I came because I wanted to be with you."

Now, a week before Mother's Day, I wasn't sure what to do.

"Call Susan up," Jenny said, "and wish her Happy Mother's Day. Or send her a card. She's only been here for two months. It's not like you owe her more than that."

"Maybe I shouldn't call her at all." It seemed a betrayal of my mother to acknowledge Susan in this way. "It's like adultery," I told Jenny.

"Come on. What did you do when your grandmothers were alive? Didn't you call them on Mother's Day?"

"That was different."

"I say 'Happy Mother's Day' to people at work. If that's your idea of adultery, then I'm the most promiscuous person you know."

I felt some obligation to Susan, if only because her other son had died. So on the Wednesday before Mother's Day, I bought her a card with the words "Happy Mother's Day" on the front and added the following note:

Dear Susan,

I'm glad I've gotten the chance to meet you. I don't know how much longer you'll be staying in San Francisco or how much time we'll spend together. Things may not be easy between us. But I'm grateful that you made the effort to find me and that we've started some kind of relationship. I hope you have a happy Mother's Day.

Affectionately,
Ben

Then I went shopping for my mother. I was compensating, spending more money on gifts than I ever had before. I bought her a maroon-and-gray silk scarf because those were the Vassar colors and she was a loyal alumna. I sent her *A Way in the World* by V. S. Naipaul because she liked reading him in *The New York Review of Books*, and *None to Accompany Me* by Nadine Gordimer because she had enjoyed *Burger's Daughter* years before and was interested in South African politics. I went to the florist and ordered a huge bouquet of flowers: red, yellow, and white roses; irises, orchids, tulips, lilies.

At school, I spoke about evolving conceptions of motherhood during the course of American history. I discussed maternity leave, glass ceilings, and the case of a woman who sued her boss because she'd been fired for nursing on the job. I asked my students what they were planning to do for Mother's Day.

"I'll make my bed," said one. "That will be my gift to my mother."

"I don't believe in Mother's Day," another student said. He had been reading *The Communist Manifesto* and had come to see everything through the eyes of Karl Marx. "It's a creation of the Hallmark industry, and as such, it's a capitalist tool."

"*You're* a tool," said a girl he'd berated for shopping at Benetton. "You celebrate Valentine's Day, don't you?"

"That's different."

"Only because you want to get laid."

"All right," I said. "Enough."

"Why are we talking about Mother's Day?" one student asked. "We're not in second grade. Are you going to give us crayons and ask us to make cards?"

"I'm not trying to treat you like children," I said. "I just think it's an interesting subject to discuss."

"You think it's a subject?"

"It *is* a subject. Mother's Day as an American phenomenon—what it says about our economy and our culture."

But what I really wanted to talk about was myself. I told my students about my Mother's Day dilemma and how I'd tried to solve it.

"Why do you keep telling us about your life?" asked one student.

"Because it touches on larger issues." Somewhere in my mind, somewhere small and receding, I realized I was talking in earnest. I'd lost my sense of humor. "For a while you guys were obsessed with my life. Don't you remember what you asked me at the beginning of the year? 'Are you married? Do you have a girlfriend?' "

"We don't want to know about your life," a student said. "We only want to know about your sex life."

"That's right," a voice called out. This was Paul. "We only want to know about your birth mother if you're having sex with her."

The room rocked with laughter—at the image of me having sex with my birth mother, or perhaps of me having sex at all, their hopelessly earnest history teacher.

At home that night, I told Jenny I was having trouble getting through to my students.

"They're teenagers, Ben. You can't expect them to be interested in this." She got up from the bed and brought back the chess set. "Here. This will relax you."

"Chess?"

The first time I'd played, when I was eight, I'd reached across the board and simply taken my father's pieces—his queen and castles, and then his king. "Beginner's luck!" I'd said.

"You have to think to play chess," I told Jenny. "That's not going to relax me."

She moved her pawn; then I moved mine. The window was open. A breeze blew across the room, billowing the Venezuelan flag, making it look like a huge life jacket. I raised an earring of Jenny's to my ear. Maybe Susan would make a pair of earrings for her. Maybe she'd make a pair for my mother. I lay on my back and closed my eyes.

"It's your turn," Jenny said.

"You go for me." I craned my neck, leaning my head off the edge of the bed so I could see the room upside down.

"What are you doing?"

I tried to read the titles on the bookshelves. I made out the name Oliver Sacks and the title *An Anthropologist on Mars*. Sacks had written about a surgeon with Tourette's syndrome and a man for whom the world had frozen in the 1960s.

When I sat up, Jenny was bending over the chessboard. Brown curls hung in front of her face. She had a bishop in each hand—one black, one white—contemplating our respective moves.

"Jen," I said, "there should be a mathematical constant—call it X—that represents the ratio of time I think about Susan to the time I actually spend with her. It would be huge."

"Call it W," Jenny said.

"W?"

"For 'waste of time.'"

I could see that the subject was starting to wear on her. She hadn't bargained for this kind of relationship.

"Call it O," she said.

"O?"

"For 'obsessed.' Or S."

"S?"

"For 'self-absorbed.' "

True to my prediction, I didn't return to synagogue services. But I thought about religion more and more. I would flip through the pages of the Bible—reading the verses and the Rashi commentary in the original Hebrew. On Fridays, I sometimes called my parents before the sun went down in New York and had my father bless me.

I introduced Jenny to traditional Jewish foods, such as smoked herring and gefilte fish. I removed my high school yearbook from storage and showed her pictures of me from the basketball team, loping down the court in my Hebrew-lettered uniform, with a monogrammed yarmulke, crocheted by a former girlfriend, bobby-pinned to my hair. I described the plays my high school class had performed—Hebrew versions of *The Wizard of Oz*, *My Fair Lady*, *Oliver!* and *The Rocky Horror Picture Show*. I taught Tara "The Time Warp" in Hebrew.

"What are you doing?" Jenny asked.

"I'm teaching Tara the pelvic thrust."

"In Hebrew?"

"Why not?"

I asked Jenny whether it was all right if we put a mezuzah on our front doorpost. "It would mean something to me, if it's okay with you."

A close childhood friend of Jenny's had grown up in a Conservative Jewish home, and Jenny had helped her nail a mezuzah to her doorpost. Jenny had no objection to our having one, as long as she understood what it meant.

I told her about the end of enslavement in Egypt, when God passed over the houses of the Israelites and killed the Egyptians' firstborns. That was what the mezuzah symbolized—the protection granted to a Jewish home.

"Except this isn't a Jewish home," Jenny said. "Only one of us is Jewish."

"Which is why I'm asking if it's all right with you. I won't do it if you object."

She didn't object. But she was less interested in what the Torah said than in what meaning the tradition had for me. Why, now, did I want a mezuzah on my doorpost? "Does it have to do with Susan?"

"That's part of it. You'd think meeting her would make me feel less Jewish. I could embrace Scottish culture—you know, raise sheep or play the bagpipes. But it's made me feel more Jewish. I can't take things for granted anymore."

There was also, I said, the issue of her.

"Me?"

"Moving in with you, Jen. That makes things more serious between us. It may sound strange, but if you were Jewish, this might not concern me as much."

"If it doesn't concern you, then why let it come between us?"

"But it does concern me. That's what I'm saying."

She was sitting across from me on the kitchen counter, her legs swinging back and forth. Next to the window hung a mesh basket with onions in it. A piece of onion skin had fallen and settled in her hair. I reached over and brushed it away.

"It's other things too," I said. "I miss the ritual. Back in college, I was making a statement by dropping everything. Why follow the laws if you don't believe in God? But I like the way I was raised. The sabbath, for example. It's nice to have a day of rest."

"You want to stop doing work on Saturdays?"

"No. But I wouldn't mind celebrating the sabbath in some form."

So Jenny and I agreed to an experiment. We'd have a sabbath dinner. There would be some ritual, but we wouldn't overdo it—no worrying about the meat's being kosher or about cooking the food before the sun went down. Although we'd sing songs and maybe make a few blessings, we wouldn't overemphasize the role of God, since none of us believed in Him.

Tara too was receptive to the experiment, perhaps because these rituals seemed exotic to her. I'd shown her the mezuzah I'd bought, along with the Hebrew text to be inserted in it. She'd pretended to read the Hebrew, babbling in a foreign accent, making nonsense guttural sounds.

I gave Jenny a book about sabbath observance, and explained to her the origins of the sabbath—that the Israelites, when wandering through the desert, were commanded by God to rest on the seventh day, that God Himself had rested on the seventh day after creating the world. The Israelites had worked on the tabernacle in the desert, and the sabbath prohibitions were related to that work. Thirty-nine types of work done in the tabernacle were forbidden to Jews on the sabbath, as were all the corollaries to those types of work.

"What about turning electricity on and off?" Jenny asked. "They didn't even have electricity back then."

She was right, I said. But the prohibition against electricity was part of the larger prohibition against work. I told her it was forbidden to carry anything on public property; you couldn't even wheel a baby carriage. Some men "wore" their keys by turning them into tie clips. I described the concept of *eruv*. If you were able to enclose public property—with a wall or even a piece of string—and if that enclosure complied with certain laws, then public property became private. My freshman year at Yale, several Jews had "purchased" Old Campus for a dollar so that they could carry on it. Even the *eruv* around Manhattan was accepted by some Orthodox Jews. Manhattan was an island, after all. It was surrounded by water.

"That sounds like a loophole," Jenny said. "What's the point of observing the sabbath if everyone's looking for ways to get around it?"

There was the letter of the law, I said, and the spirit of the law. Everything depended on the reason behind it. If you could find a loophole in a law in order more fully to observe the sabbath, then why not use it? My father had put the lights on a timer so that they were on when we were awake and off when we were asleep; that way we wouldn't have to sit in the dark. But he refused to use a timer for the stereo or TV. "There are loopholes," I told Jenny, "and then there are loopholes."

"What about the *shabbes goy*?" Jenny was fascinated by the idea that Jews could ask non-Jews to do work for them. What was the difference between doing work yourself and having someone else do it for you?

If you had a non-Jew purchase clothes for you, I said, if you had that person turn on the TV or CD player, then you surely weren't adhering to the spirit of the sabbath. But there were good reasons to use a *shabbes goy*.

"Like what?"

"To wheel your infant to synagogue."

"I don't see the difference," Jenny said. "If you're asking someone to do work for you, you might as well do it yourself. And what difference does it make if the person's not Jewish?"

"Jews are commanded to observe the sabbath. If you ask a Jew to break the sabbath you're getting that person to sin."

"You believe that?"

"No. But this isn't about what I believe."

"What's it about, then? And how about your father? Lots of his colleagues must be secular Jews. Does he think of them as sinners?

Would he ask me to turn off a light on the sabbath, but not one of them?"

"Jen," I said, "I can't explain my father. He probably can't explain himself either. But yes, that's what he'd probably do."

She read the books I'd given her and asked me questions when she didn't understand. I did my best to answer her. I'm not a rabbi. I have a good memory, but I've forgotten some things over the years. She took seriously this crash course in Judaism, but she was also ironic about it. She became a fount of hypothetical questions, rivaling my philosophy professors at Yale, rivaling the rabbis of the Talmud in her pursuit of counterfactuals.

"Let's say you wake up," she said, "and you're riding in a taxi on the sabbath."

"How's that possible?"

"What if you're on the way home from work and you get stuck in a traffic jam and it gets dark?"

"Then you get out and walk."

"What if you're in an airplane?"

"Are you asking me if you jump?"

"Yes."

I laughed. "No, Jen, you don't jump."

She was curious about Judaism, but she's a curious person. She'd be as interested in learning Hindu practices or in picking up a few words of Swahili. Perhaps if I'd talked more about these rituals when we'd met, what was happening now would have made sense to her. But my interest was sudden—related, she suspected, to my having met Susan. On her mother's side, Jenny's family could be traced back to the *Mayflower*. But we didn't reenact early American rituals. Jenny didn't dress up as a Pilgrim.

Still, she looked forward to our sabbath meal. I wrote out the blessings over the wine and challah in transliterated Hebrew. I did the same for a couple of sabbath songs, and taught them to her and Tara.

The day of our sabbath meal, I came home after school and cooked. I showered and put on a dress shirt and slacks. Jenny and Tara had showered too, and were wearing skirts and blouses. Jenny had on a touch of makeup.

"You two look beautiful," I said. I kissed them each on the cheek.

Jenny said the blessing on the sabbath candles, placing her hands over her eyes and repeating the Hebrew words after me.

We sat down at the table, where I recited the kiddush. Between courses, we sang the songs I'd transliterated. Jenny and Tara caught on quickly to the tunes. It reminded me of Friday nights when I was younger, when I knew there was nothing else I could do besides sit and spend time with my family.

"This is nice," Jenny said.

I agreed. "You don't even have to think of it as religious." I wasn't sure whom I was saying this for—Jenny, Tara, or myself.

"It kind of *is* religious," Tara said.

"But you don't have to be religious to participate," I said. "And it's only a small part of the meal. It's really just a chance to think."

"Are you becoming religious?" Tara asked me. She looked down at the transliterated Hebrew.

"Not really."

"Because I like you the way you are. Most of the time. And it's my home. I was here a long time before you."

"That's true."

"So you can't just show up and change things."

Jenny rested her hand on Tara's arm. "Ben and I asked you if it was okay if we did this."

Tara didn't respond.

"And you agreed. We wouldn't have had this meal if you didn't want us to."

"This better not be the beginning of something else."

"Like what?" Jenny asked.

"Whatever religious people do. Sacrificing animals."

I laughed. "There will be no animal sacrifices. I can promise you that."

"And I'm not interested in being a Jew."

"No one's asking you to be one," Jenny said.

"Or a Christian either."

"Or a Christian."

"Or a Jew for Jesus, or anything, Mom."

"What did you think?" I asked Jenny when we were doing the dishes.

"I liked it. It felt festive."

"Jen—if, hypothetically, I asked you to convert, would you consider it?"

"Why, hypothetically, might you ask me to do that?"

"You know what I mean. If we were going to stay together for a while—maybe even forever."

"You mean get married?"

"Sure."

"Say the word 'marriage,' Ben. It isn't going to kill you. It's not like I'm pressuring you to marry me. God knows we have things to work out."

"All right," I said, "what if we got married? Would you think about converting?" If Jenny had been Jewish, we'd have avoided some of the controversy we had that night. I'd also have avoided disappointing my parents. But I couldn't live for my parents. It was unreasonable to ask Jenny to convert for them, especially since they'd made little effort to get to know her. Converting would make things easier for our children. They wouldn't be confused about who they were. But Jenny and I hadn't even discussed children. Who knew whether we wanted to have them? I could have asked her to convert for me—I *was* asking her, wasn't I?—because Judaism was important to me. But why did it have to be important to her too? We were different in many ways; you don't look for a clone in a lover. Perhaps religion was an excuse to avoid contemplating the future. I was still spinning my wheels, convinced more than ever that something had to happen before I could think in those terms. Maybe this too was an excuse, and I was suffering from something as banal as an inability to commit.

"You heard what Tara said. She's not interested in being Jewish."

"I'm not talking about Tara. I'm talking about us, Jen—you and me."

"I'm talking about us too. Really, Ben, think about it. You wouldn't want me to go through a sham conversion just to make things easier. I'm not religious, and I never will be. And I didn't grow up with Jewish culture, so I'll never be Jewish in that way. I liked dinner tonight. I'd be glad to do it again. But I'm interested in it because of you—because you said it was part of who you are."

"Well, it is."

"And that's enough of a reason for me. But it's your religion and your culture, not mine. Nothing's going to change that."

Jenny had more pressing things on her mind than the question of converting to Judaism. She'd been a public defender for six years and was busier than before at work. She'd gone from working on misdemeanors to defending felony criminals, many of them violent. She'd gained respect in her office, winning cases no one thought she could win, plea-bargaining successfully on numerous occasions so that her clients were given probation or short sentences when they had expected to spend years in jail.

I was struck by her aplomb. She was always professional, never grandstanding, simply doing her job. Jenny is calm when most people wouldn't be—when I, certainly, wouldn't be.

But when I came home one evening at the end of May, I found her sprawled across our bed, looking anything but calm.

"What's wrong?"

"I got assigned a rape case."

"So?"

"Ben, I'm going to be defending a rapist."

"An alleged rapist, you mean." *Alleged* was Jenny's favorite word. She could cite examples of forced confession, police brutality, and tampered evidence; jurors sometimes followed their prejudices and disregarded the orders of the judge. She could list the names of people who had been wrongfully convicted—defendants later proven innocent, some of them too late, they'd already been executed. At her insistence, we'd rented *A Thin Blue Line*, even though I'd already seen it once and she'd seen it three times. She stopped the tape again and again, pointing to the ways the state used its power, all the forces aligned against the suspect.

Through a combination of luck and careful maneuvering, she'd avoided getting assigned any rape cases. But now that she had risen within the office, it had become simply a matter of time. She told me she'd considered trying to get off the case, but how could she justify doing that? She hadn't been raped. If she had, she might have been more eager to take on the case, to prove that she'd overcome what had happened to her.

"I met him today," she said, "and he gave me the creeps."

"The creeps?" This didn't sound like her.

"When I saw the guy leering at me, all I could think was, Get me off this case—I don't want to have anything to do with you." Jenny was doing laps around the room, cogitating, ruminating, like a basketball coach, not knowing where to direct her energy. "I kept thinking, Your fingerprints match, you don't have an alibi, and the semen's at the lab and I have no doubt it will match. Just cop a plea. Don't sully me with this."

Jenny's freshman roommate at U.C. Berkeley had been raped by a stranger in an alley off campus. She'd dropped out of school and gone home to Missouri. As far as Jenny knew, she'd never recovered. "That guy ruined her life," Jenny told me once.

Still, that was fourteen years before. Lots of criminals ruined their victims' lives; Jenny knew that. She'd heard hundreds of victims testify in court; she'd seen their families hold vigil; she wasn't insensitive to what crime did to them. But if she was always thinking about the victims, she wouldn't have been able to do her job. She could have chosen to be a prosecutor. Or she could have taken the easy route and worked for a law firm, making a good salary and avoiding many hard questions.

"Don't you think he has the right to a good defense?" I asked. Then I felt bad, throwing her argument back at her.

"Rape is different." On the nightstand was a picture of Jenny holding Tara hours after she was born. Jenny was still in college. I saw that picture every day, but it struck me now, perhaps because Jenny looked so young. One moment you were in college, the next you were a mother, and the next you were defending violent criminals in court. How did that all fit together? Was there a moment when you realized that your decisions had consequences, that other people's lives depended on you?

"Why's it different?"

"It just is. It's something you can't understand."

"Don't tell me it's a woman's thing."

"It *is* a woman's thing. Do you understand what it's like to walk alone at night and know you could be raped?"

"Not the way you do, obviously. But I can try to imagine it."

"That doesn't compare."

Did she understand what it was like to wonder where you came from, to spend your whole life staring at strangers, thinking, He looks like me, so does she? We could compete over untranslatable experiences, deciding that no one understood anyone else and we should talk only to ourselves. "If rape is a woman's thing," I said, "then robbery is a property owner's thing and pederasty is a child's thing. Where does that leave empathy?"

"Rape's just different. I can't explain it."

That might have been the end of the conversation, but when Jenny and I went to visit Jonathan and Sandy, I made the mistake of mentioning Jenny's case. Jonathan asked her if she'd become less high-minded.

"Don't even start," Jenny said. I didn't know what it was about Jenny and Jonathan. They liked each other. But she could make him defensive, perhaps because she fought the battle he used to fight, back in college when he was political. "I'm going to defend this guy."

"So we're back to where we began—you defending absolutely anyone."

"Come on," Sandy said. "Leave Jenny alone."

"Tell me something," Jenny said to Jonathan, "do you go through your patients' tax records to see if they've cheated? Do you ask them whether they beat their wives or whether they've been arrested?"

"No."

"That's what I thought. You don't say, 'Sorry, Mr. Mengele, no stool sample from you,' or, 'Excuse me, ma'am, but do you love your children—and if you don't, I can't give you a CAT scan.'"

"I took an oath when I graduated from medical school to help heal the sick."

"I took an oath too."

"Everyone's entitled to medical care."

"They're also entitled to legal counsel."

Jonathan wasn't convinced. After Jenny left to get Tara, he continued the argument with me. "What would Jenny do if Sandy or I got beaten up? It happens all the time—kids with baseball bats kicking the shit out of gays. What if Jenny were hired to defend the guy?"

"That's absurd," I said. "The odds are so small you'd do better to buy a lottery ticket. Besides, Jenny wouldn't be allowed to take the case. It would be a conflict of interests."

"I think she does good work," Sandy said.

Jonathan ignored him. "Don't get me wrong, Ben. I like Jenny. But sometimes it gets to me. You've chosen such a do-gooder girlfriend. It's like you've married Mom."

"She's not Mom, and I haven't married her. And what's wrong with being a do-gooder? You're a do-gooder yourself. What do you think being a doctor is?"

He didn't answer me. "Why can't you chart a new path for once?"

Chart a new path? I'd met my birth mother. True, she'd contacted me first, but I hadn't refused to meet her, as Jonathan would have done with his. I wasn't afraid of my past. Did he think that because he was gay he was more of a man than I was, that he'd grown up and I hadn't?

When I got home, I found Jenny on our bed with her knees up and her shoes off, thin bands of dirt like zebra stripes along the tops of her feet. She'd changed into a black tank top and a long gingham skirt with a flower print across it. Her hair was tied back. "You look beautiful," I said.

"Your brother was a prick today."

"I'm sorry. I shouldn't have brought the subject up."

"It's not your fault." She rolled over on her stomach and asked me to give her a massage. I rubbed her back, shoulders, and neck.

"I need a vacation," she said.

"I do too."

"We should go somewhere. We haven't taken a vacation together in over a year."

"Vacations are expensive."

"I'm not talking about something fancy. Just a chance for us to get away for a while."

I thought about this the next day at work, and when I came home that night, I told Jenny that I'd take her on a vacation when Tara left for summer camp.

"I didn't mean take me. We can go in on it together."

"I *want* to take you. You can get a couple of days off work. We'll go down the coast, maybe stay at a bed-and-breakfast."

When I went with Susan to see *Apollo 13*, she'd suggested that she meet Jonathan, Jenny, and Tara. She'd been patient, she said. She also thought it was a good idea for us to spend time together with other people around. As things stood, too much was at stake when we saw each other alone. We were having trouble relaxing.

She may have been right, but it bothered me how she approached our relationship—as something to work on, to construct. Her casualness was willed, which made it not casual.

But now, a month later, with Jenny apprehensive about her work, I thought that getting together with Susan might distract her. Also, my parents were coming to visit the next week, and Susan wanted to meet them too. I wasn't prepared for that to happen. So Susan and I made an agreement. She could meet Jonathan, Jenny, and Tara, but not my parents.

When we met, Susan was wearing a yellow cotton pantsuit that made her look like someone who belonged at a Miami Beach resort. The rest of us were in jeans and sneakers. It was a Sunday. We'd agreed to have brunch at Noah's Bagels on Irving Street, where bicyclists in Lycra shorts stopped in to pick up sandwiches, and teenagers holding skateboards tasted the lox trim with no intention of buying it. Susan looked out of place, and by association, we did as well.

There was a series of handshakes, all of us sticking our arms across one another's bodies, as if we were engaged in some sort of dance, reaching into the circle.

"It's nice to meet you," Susan told everyone.

We ordered bagel sandwiches from the counter and sat down at a table. The space was too small. We sat huddled, our legs bumping, a profusion of apologies uttered as if we all were strangers.

"Well," I said.

"Well," said Susan.

I'd had no expectations for this meal, nothing other than the hope that everyone would get along. Now, however, as we all sat in silence, I thought of myself as a host who had brought together the wrong combination of people. I felt responsible, but more than that. I wanted everyone to like Susan, not, principally, because I liked her, but because I considered her an extension of me.

Jenny said that the weather was good.

Jonathan agreed.

It *was* good, but no better than yesterday and no better, in all likelihood, than it would be tomorrow. It was June in San Francisco; the weather was always good in June. I wished for a hailstorm, something remarkable for us to discuss. Maybe that was why there were so many boring people in California. They always talked about the weather, which hardly ever changed. *It's sunny out. It certainly is.*

Tara had her face low to the table. She was concentrating on her bagel. She seemed oblivious of the rest of us. She could as easily have been eating alone.

"I'm glad to meet you," Susan said again. She was talking to all three of them.

Jenny smiled and gently nudged Tara, to get her to look up. "We're glad to meet you too," Jenny said.

Jonathan seemed about to reach out and shake Susan's hand. Had he forgotten we'd done that already? "How do you like San Francisco?" he asked.

"I like it a lot. And you?"

"Me?" Jonathan said.

"Do you like San Francisco?"

"Oh. Yes. But I've lived here for a while."

Susan took another bite. But no sooner had she done that than she put her bagel down again, seeming to want to speak. It was as if she hadn't yet learned how to coordinate these activities. I pictured her epiglottis, flipping back and forth as she ate and talked, victim of her indecision, trying to keep up with her brain.

"You're Ben's brother." She appeared simply to be musing, talking to herself as much as to anyone else. Over her shoulder, in a big plastic box attached to the counter, mini-hamantaschen were arranged in piles: prune, apricot, and cherry; they looked like pieces of candy. On the wall opposite the counter were photographs of Noah and of his parents. There were pictures of New Yorkers protesting the Brooklyn Dodgers' move to L.A. and of David Ben-Gurion talking with Albert Einstein. There were handwritten letters from satisfied customers, including one from somebody who had been born in Eastern Europe and grown up in New York City, and who said Noah's bagels compared favorably with any other bagels in the world. I imagined a bagel store in Indiana, golden-haired farm kids smiling pleasantly at you as they tossed frozen Lender's into the microwave.

"You're adopted also," Susan said to Jonathan. This came out like an announcement.

Jonathan looked amused. "That's right."

This too provoked silence.

Periodically, Jenny and Jonathan looked at Susan. They were curious about her, glad enough to be here, I could tell—even my brother, who'd pretended that having to come to brunch had been an imposition on him. But they didn't say anything to Susan. I felt like a talk-show host, with the urge to introduce her to the audience. *This is my birth mother, folks—what do you think?*

"I'm sorry," Susan told them. "The last thing I want is to make everyone uncomfortable."

"It's just an unusual situation," I said. "I mean, you and me being related, Susan, but not really. And Jonathan and me also being related but not really, but in the opposite way that you and I are. It's kind of like Jack Sprat."

Everyone stared at me perplexedly.

"You know," I said. "Jack Sprat and his wife. One of them ate fat and the other ate lean. But together, they ate everything—they covered all the bases." I stared at my plate with the confusion of someone who had never seen a bagel before. "Then there's me and Jenny. We're not even related at all."

Now Susan came to *my* rescue. "I've heard a lot about you," she told the three of them.

"Like what?" Jonathan asked. Was he pleased to hear this, or did he wish that I hadn't talked about him with someone he considered a stranger? The fact was, I hadn't said much about him or Jenny; my conversations with Susan had focused mostly on us. But I had told her that Jonathan was gay. Was that what she was referring to? I hadn't prepared anyone for what would happen today. I should have done a better job of prompting them.

Susan spoke to Jonathan. "I've actually seen you several times before."

"You have?"

She told him what she'd told me—that she'd grown up in New Jersey, and that when we were children she used to ride across the bridge and watch the two of us play in Riverside Park.

"You spied on us?" Jonathan glared at me, as if I were implicated in what Susan had done.

"I wasn't spying." Susan seemed to regret having brought this up. "I just wanted to watch Ben play."

Susan turned to Jenny. "Ben tells me you're a public defender. And that you've just gotten a rape case."

"Mom's feeling conflicted about rape," Tara said. She appeared simply to be mouthing the words, amused to hear the phrase—*Mom's feeling conflicted*—come out, as if she were mimicking something she'd read.

"I'm not feeling conflicted about rape," Jenny said. "When it comes to rape, there's nothing to feel conflicted about."

"She's feeling conflicted about *defending* a rapist."

"Yes," Jenny said. "Well . . ."

Susan listed some things she'd heard about the three of them. She knew that Jonathan was a doctor and that Jenny had gone to U.C. Berkeley and Stanford Law School. She mentioned Tara's pottery lessons. These were trivial facts, but they made it appear that Susan was showing off. In a way she was. I was beginning to understand that she liked to inform you she knew about you. That had been one of the purposes of her hiring a private detective—to fluster me. Now she was flustering Jonathan and Jenny as well.

She had another purpose, I suspected. She hoped that by listing all the things she knew, she might get Jenny and Jonathan to reciprocate. She wanted to determine what they knew about her. Was she an important part of my life? Was I talking about her with them? Rattled by her list of facts, Jonathan and Jenny didn't tell her much. They ate their bagels in relative silence.

Finally Jenny spoke. "It must have been hard having a baby at sixteen."

Susan looked surprised.

"I had Tara at twenty-one," Jenny said. "It's not sixteen, but I was still just a kid."

"It was my own fault," Susan said. "I'm the one who got pregnant."

"Maybe so. But I assume someone else was involved. You're the one who had to live with the consequences."

"Except I didn't. I gave Ben up." Susan looked sadly at Tara. I guessed she was imagining me at that age, wondering what her life would have been like if she'd kept me.

"I was five years older than you were," Jenny said. "That makes all the difference in the world. I had a husband for a while. I was practically done with college."

"Still," Susan said. "Maybe—" But she didn't finish her thought. She said nothing more, and neither did anyone else. We all sat quietly eating.

When we got home, I felt disappointed, as if I'd promised a good time and hadn't delivered, as if everything Susan had said reflected poorly on me.

"That was your birth mother?" Tara said. "The person you've been flipping out over?"

"I haven't been flipping out over her." I folded my arms across my chest.

"You've been turning your life upside down. That's what Mom says, and I agree."

"Didn't you like Susan?"

"She was all right. She could have been bigger or smarter or something."

I thought of telling Tara that when I'd met Susan I too had been disappointed by how ordinary she'd seemed. But I didn't see the point of it. "Everyone was tense. You might like her more next time."

We were in Tara's bedroom. The shades were drawn, and the light from the fish tank cast the room in the blue hues of an aquarium. Facedown on Tara's bed was a copy of *Little Women*. "I liked that book," I said, "but I didn't read it until I was in high school. You're a lot more advanced than I was. A lot smarter." She lay down on her bed and started to read. "Tell me something," I said, "was it wrong of me to ask you to come along today?"

"It wasn't wrong . . ."

"But?"

"Susan didn't even talk to me."

"We were all nervous. You probably handled it better than we did."

"Well, I don't want to see her again."

My father had known for almost a year that he was coming to lecture at U.C. Berkeley. But only in the last month had my mother decided to join him. I suspected this had to do with Susan's arrival. My mother was looking for an excuse to visit.

My parents arrived in San Francisco on a Thursday night. Jonathan was on call, so I greeted them alone at the airport.

"It's great to be here," my mother said.

I smiled at her and took her in my arms, pressing her tightly against me.

My father stepped forward and kissed me on the cheek. "You look good, Ben."

"Thanks, Dad. You do too."

He ran his fingers through my hair, then kissed me again, this time on the other cheek—two kisses, the way the French did.

My mother wheeled a suitcase across the floor and my father clutched his briefcase. He carried it with him wherever he went. Years before, I'd imagined he purveyed secret information—my father the spy, the carrier of some code, everywhere toting his secrets.

"Dad and I flew together," my mother said. They'd flown separately when Jonathan and I were children, so that if one of them was killed in a crash the other could take care of us. For years I'd worried that this would happen; I wasn't sure which parent I hoped would survive.

"The whole thing was silly," my father said now.

"I was worried about the boys," said my mother.

"I was too. But if we really were worried, we should have taken separate taxis and flown together. The cab ride's the most dangerous part of the trip."

"Everything worked out in the end."

"That's true." I heard contrition in my father's voice, felt his desire to protect Jonathan and me. We walked quietly through the airport corridors, out to where my car was parked.

The next day, Jonathan took my father on his patient rounds. I had no classes after lunch, so my mother and I visited Jenny at work.

Jenny and my mother traded statistics about the death penalty—specifically about how it was racially biased. If the murder victim was white, Jenny said, the suspect was more likely to be sentenced to death. All else being equal, black defendants received the death penalty at higher rates than whites did.

"I know," my mother said. "You don't even have to worry about the Eighth Amendment. It's a problem already with the Fourteenth Amendment." Their interaction was so casual a stranger might have thought I was the boyfriend and they were mother and daughter.

As if further to establish her authority, my mother gave a breakdown of Supreme Court opinions. Only Justices Brennan and Marshall, she said, considered the death penalty a violation of the prohibition on cruel and unusual punishment, although Justice Blackmun, over time, had come to oppose it on due-process grounds. "But Marshall's dead, and Brennan and Blackmun are gone from the Court. Which doesn't leave the country in a very good position."

Jenny showed my mother her office, which she shared with another public defender. Next to Jenny's computer were two photographs, one of Tara and one of me. Political buttons were pinned to the bulletin board. "Impeach Ronald Reagan." "Don't ask, don't tell, don't get it." "Adlai Stevenson in '52."

"I campaigned for Stevenson," my mother told Jenny.

"You did?"

"I used to go door-to-door for him. Maybe it's because I was just a teenager and you feel things most strongly when you're young, but to this day I still think he's the best candidate we ever had. The world would have been a much better place if he'd beaten Eisenhower."

Jenny handed my mother the Stevenson button. "You can have it," she said.

My mother smiled gratefully, but stuck it back on the bulletin board. "I wouldn't want to take it from you." She stared at the tiny picture on the button. "Stevenson had a strange effect on a lot of people. We related to him as much more than a candidate. Ben's father feels the same way about Dean Acheson. Acheson was the only person he thought was qualified to be president."

"But Acheson never ran," Jenny said.

"That's all the more reason Ben's father liked him. He thinks that wanting to be president automatically disqualifies you. I tend to agree."

I stood next to them by Jenny's desk. Yet I was removed, watching from a distance as they talked to each other.

Jenny and my mother had gotten along, but later that afternoon, when my father returned to the hotel, I had to ask my parents why they hadn't invited Jenny to sabbath dinner, which we would have in their suite that evening.

"If we'd known it was important to you," my mother said, "we would have. But then we'd have had to invite Tara as well."

"So what?"

"It would have changed the flavor of everything. We're only here for the weekend. Dad and I thought it would be nice to spend the sabbath just with the family."

"But Jenny *is* family."

"No she isn't," my father said. "She's your girlfriend. You've had girlfriends before, and you may have others in the future."

"I live with Jenny."

"I know you do. But that doesn't mean the two of you are married. You could move to New York. There are lots of single Jewish women there."

"I'm not interested in single Jewish women. I'm interested in Jenny. Besides, I live here. This is where my job is."

"There are jobs in New York."

"There are jobs in Thailand too, but I'm not moving there. Dad, listen to me. I live with Jenny. I wake up with her every morning. I go to sleep with her at night. I help raise her daughter. You may be my family—"

"We may be?"

"You are, Dad. Of course." I resented having to insist on this, resented that my parents were probably thinking about Susan, whom, to my surprise, they hadn't yet mentioned on this trip. But this didn't have anything to do with Susan. Whether or not I'd met her, I'd have hoped my parents would invite Jenny to dinner.

"Besides," my father said, "Jenny isn't Jewish. What would she do at a sabbath dinner? She'd be uncomfortable, and so would we."

"She wouldn't be uncomfortable. In fact, we had our own sabbath dinner last month."

"You did?" my mother said.

I might have expected my parents to be pleased—my father especially. But he didn't express pleasure. He may have taken this as evidence that my relationship with Jenny was more serious than he'd thought.

"We didn't invite Sandy either," he said.

"Well, you should have," I said, although I knew that Sandy wouldn't have come. Not because he'd have objected to coming but because my brother would have wanted it that way. Jonathan compartmentalized. He kept his life with Sandy and his life with my parents as distinct as possible.

"It's just sabbath dinner," my father said. "It's not a convention. Did you expect us to invite your birth mother as well?"

"Of course not."

"Not everything has to be all-inclusive, Ben."

"I know, Dad. It just would have been nice for you guys to invite her."

Jonathan came to the hotel and helped us prepare for the sabbath. We set the table in the common area with a tablecloth my father had brought from New York. My mother was out walking in Golden Gate Park.

"Dad brought everything," Jonathan said. "He doesn't think there are stores in San Francisco."

"That's not true," my father said. He sniffed the roses he'd bought for my mother. I liked thinking of him those sabbaths he was away, calling card in hand in hotel rooms around the world, sending flowers to her.

He put the challahs on the table and laid out the utensils. Soon my mother returned, hurrying through the suite with her coat trailing behind her. She sliced carrots while my father shaved in the bathroom; he called out instructions about what lights to leave on. Friday afternoons when I was a child, I stood on the toilet seat so I could look him in the eye, and reached out to feel his stubble.

"I'm glad you're here," I said, standing next to him in the bathroom.

"Me too." Outside, the sun was descending; he looked at his

watch to see how long until sunset. "Do you remember when you were small, and you thought daylight saving time was just for Jews? You thought non-Jews didn't move their clocks forward."

"I think so," I answered.

"It was sweet. It's something I'll remember for the rest of my life."

I stood beside him while my mother lit the candles. When he finished praying he blessed Jonathan and me. He held his hands above our heads and moved his lips slowly. I could feel his breath as he whispered in our ears.

At dinner, I joined him as he sang the sabbath songs. My mother hummed along, while Jonathan stayed quiet. I thought of a time when God watched over me, when he appeared in my dreams with his long gray beard.

After dinner, I went into the bedroom. I opened the blinds and looked down at the city. The streetlights cast shadows across Golden Gate Park.

On the nightstand lay my father's tefillin. He placed them on his head and wrapped them around his arm when he prayed at home every weekday morning. In the tefillin boxes lay the words of God. I'd once wanted nothing more than to reach my bar mitzvah so I could wrap the tefillin around my arm.

A prayer book was tucked inside the tefillin sack, along with a crocheted yarmulke big enough to stay on my father's head without the help of a bobby pin. He'd lost most of his hair over the years. I took out the prayer book and began to recite the sabbath evening service.

A few minutes later, Jonathan walked in. He was on his way to the bathroom.

"What are you doing?"

"Praying," I said.

"Ben, I don't get it."

"What?"

He took a step toward me and pointed at the prayer book. "This."

"It's the sabbath, and Mom and Dad are here." I thought about the Millsteins, my parents' made-up friends, and how you could be Jewish in name only. What was the point of being that kind of Jew?

"Ben, you're thirty years old. You're too young to be nostalgic."

I didn't say anything.

"You're becoming religious again, aren't you?"

"No."

"You consult a rabbi. You and Jenny celebrate the sabbath. You're standing in the dark, praying. Why are you doing all this?"

"It's a lot of things. Susan's coming to town. My finding out I wasn't born Jewish. Things getting more serious with Jenny. Maybe it's the fact that I'm growing older. We're not kids anymore."

"I know we're not. That's why we stopped being religious. It's what we did when we were young, because we didn't know any different. But I look at you now, and I see you reverting."

"I'm not reverting, I assure you."

"What are you doing, then? Sometimes I have no clue who you are. I just don't understand you."

The next morning, while my father was in synagogue, I walked with my mother through Golden Gate Park. We strolled past the Arboretum and the de Young Museum, then circled back through the Haight.

"I'd like to have been here in the sixties," my mother said.

"It's still the sixties here."

"No it's not. It's a bunch of teenagers pretending it's the sixties, a lot of whom know nothing about politics. They don't even remember who Ho Chi Minh was."

"How could they? They weren't even born."

In the summer of 1963, my mother went south with my father and registered voters. Two summers later she went south again, holding Jonathan and me, a baby in each arm, and knocked on doors in Montgomery, Alabama. With all her heart she believed in equality. She'd wanted to name her children after the murdered civil rights workers Andrew Goodman, James Chaney, and Michael Schwerner, but my father insisted on biblical names.

"Why not name them after someone we care about?" she said.

"I care about the Bible," my father answered. "These are the people I've dreamed about all my life."

"What about the people *I* dream about?"

But in the end, she relented. She knew when to pick her fights with my father.

I put my arm around her. Her hair was still long, although it now had streaks of gray. Her shoulders had grown sharp and pointy. She'd always been thin, and she'd become even thinner over the years. I could probably pick her up. This thought made me feel protective of her. I looked down at her slender wrists, the silver bracelets jangling against her arms.

We stopped in front of a café on Haight Street. "Can I buy you a cup of coffee?" she asked. It was the sabbath; you weren't supposed to spend money. But when my mother wasn't with my father, she didn't observe the sabbath, and she knew I didn't observe it either. Her offer was like a bond between us, something forbidden and exciting. When my father was my age he'd already fought in a war. He'd captured a battalion of Germans. He'd lived his own life, and now I lived mine. So why did I feel that I was betraying him?

"You get coffee," I told my mother, "and I'll just sit with you and talk."

After she finished her coffee, we climbed the hills of Cole Valley, up to Ashbury Heights and over to the Castro near Jonathan and Sandy's house. We walked to Twenty-fourth Street and turned east. Boys were playing basketball in the playgrounds. Off Valencia Street the taquerías were full. The sidewalks were crowded, car exhaust was in the air, and my mother and I were simply walking, with no particular direction, it seemed, until I realized we were in the middle of the Mission, a few blocks from where Susan lived. Maybe I was tempting fate. What if we bumped into her?

Perhaps my mother felt this herself. "You know," she said, "you haven't talked much about your birth mother."

"I guess she just hasn't come up."

"Do you still see her?" I detected a note in her voice—distress, derision, I couldn't tell what. She asked the question as though Susan were an affliction I couldn't get rid of. *Do you still have athlete's foot?*

"Yes."

"What are you hoping to find out?"

"I'm not hoping to find out anything. That's not what this relationship is about."

"What's it about, then? Dad and I talk about this sometimes. We assumed that by now the novelty would have worn off."

"The novelty? You act like this is a hobby, Mom—like I've picked up stamp collecting or something. You know, Susan's had a hard life. She had another son, and he died in a car crash."

"He did? When?"

"Last year. That's what led her to find me. He wasn't even twenty-one yet."

"That's awful." My mother took my hand in an almost reflexive gesture. She said nothing more, but I sensed that she was shaken. Was she simply a bleeding heart, susceptible to anyone who suffered? Or was it something that, as a nonparent, I couldn't understand: that anyone who's had a child, especially parents like my own, who went through so much in order to bring up children, will always relate to the loss of a child as something deeply personal?

The next day was my father's lecture. We all sat in the audience: Jenny, Tara, and I, Sandy and Jonathan, my mother in the middle, the matriarch.

My father was lecturing on the collapse of the Soviet Union. I realized halfway through that I didn't know what he was saying. I'd been concentrating on the sound of his voice, watching his hands rest gently on the lectern.

"Russia," he said. I thought of White Russia, where his parents were born, and of a map he'd once drawn for me that chronicled his ancestors' travels. He had notes on the lectern, but he barely referred to them, delivering his speech without hesitation, talking in full paragraphs. I'd taken a Soviet history course at Yale, a huge survey lecture in which the professor referred on numerous occasions to "Suskind"; the name came out of his mouth with such ease and familiarity he might have been referring to a national hero. Every time he mentioned my father's name, a smile came across my face.

That evening, I drove my parents to the airport. I could see my mother's shadow in the rearview mirror slide across the vinyl. She hummed a tune I didn't recognize. I listened to it and tried to hum along.

I pictured my parents landing at Kennedy. I imagined flying ahead of them and greeting them there, the way they'd sent me letters when I left for summer camp, letters that arrived before I did. There was something about airports that made me sad. On my own trips to places far away—even in cities where there was no one I knew—I imagined someone would be there to greet me.

My father rested his hand on my back. "Ben," he said. He wanted to tell me something, I was sure, but couldn't find the words to say it.

When I got home from work the following day, Sandy called and asked me to join him on his window-washing route. He had a late-afternoon job and wanted to talk to me.

It was the last week of school, and my students had been busy with their oral reports. They'd become interested in my experiment; at last they seemed engaged. This pleased me, but my part of the work—reading their papers, preparing final grades—had tired me out. When I got home that day, I wanted to relax and spend time with Jenny and Tara. In two weeks, Tara was going to sleep-away camp for the first time, and although I told Jenny I was looking forward to our privacy, I was already beginning to miss Tara.

"Is everything all right?" I asked Sandy over the phone. Was someone sick? Sandy had looked fine at my father's lecture. So had Jonathan. He seemed a little thin, but he always had; now I was scared. It wasn't like Sandy to ask to talk to me.

When I arrived, though, Sandy looked relaxed. He handed me two squeegees, a bucket, and a pair of black rubber boots. He'd parked his small truck across the street. It was bright yellow, with the name WIPER-UP printed in black.

We walked down Church Street, our tools bumping against our jeans. People waved at Sandy, and he waved back. He was a familiar figure around the city, with his blond ponytail and his wide frame, his tools jangling from his belt. Motorists would see him hanging from a window, and they would honk at him and wave.

"I'm not hanging from any windows," I said.

"All right. I may make you climb up a ladder, but nothing above the second floor."

We washed the windows of a bakery on Church and of a sushi restaurant down the block from it. You'd think washing windows would be easy, but the body takes a while to adjust. Sandy moved the squeegee like a painter's brush, his gestures graceful and fluid. I needed to learn how much water to use and how to move my hands with the right rhythm.

Next we washed the windows of an apartment building on Valencia; I worked on the ground floor while Sandy climbed several stories and reappeared, dangling from the window by a thick metal belt. He waved at me, then pretended to lose his balance, his arms and legs splayed, like someone being pushed into a swimming pool. "Catch me if I fall!" he shouted.

When we were done washing, we sat on the hood of his truck, drying off in the sun. Sandy laid his tool belt across the hood and stretched out on his back. "I've been thinking about you," he said. "You never told me what it was like to meet your birth mother."

"It's been complicated," I said. "Has Jonathan talked to you about it?"

"Not really. He barely even talks about his own adoption."

"We used to speak about it all the time when we were kids. But then he stopped. It seemed like a conscious decision."

"I remember when he told me that he was adopted. He was so casual about it."

"He changed a lot in college. Around the time he came out, he withdrew from the family."

Sandy fingered the edges of his tool belt. "You know, I'd never have guessed that you and Jonathan were adopted. For all your differences, you're a lot like your parents."

"I guess . . ."

"It's funny, but I used to think I was adopted. My parents even joked about it. They said they must have switched babies in the hospital. But I was different from everyone in my hometown."

"Always?"

"For as long as I can remember. When I came out in high school, my parents accepted it pretty well. Nothing surprised them any longer. They wouldn't have been shocked if I'd told them I was from Neptune."

"Still, it must have been hard. They're your parents, after all."

"Sure. There are things I wish we could talk about. We hardly ever speak on the phone. It's not the way it is with you two and your parents. But there's a strong bond between us."

A pigeon alighted on the car in front of us and picked at a morsel of bread. The Muni trolley passed across the street, the orange-and-white cars clanking along the track, heading toward Noe Valley.

"I look at you," Sandy said, "and I see Jonathan." He rested his hands on his lap. They were big, the skin pale even in warm weather; beneath the skin you could see his veins. "Your brother may have changed in college, but he still cares about the family."

"I know he does."

"Look how hard he works. He's so obviously your parents' son. Your father's books are on his desk. Even his decision to go into geriatrics had a lot to do with your father."

"Is that why you wanted to talk to me?"

Sandy nodded. "Jonathan told me about your argument in the hotel room."

"It wasn't a big deal."

"Maybe not, but he feels bad about it. He should tell you himself, but he won't. Sometimes he can fly off the handle."

"We all can."

"I'm not even sure why I'm telling you this."

"I thought you were going to say that something was wrong with you guys."

"Wrong?"

"Like that one of you was sick. Maybe problems in your relationship."

"Nothing's wrong. I just wanted you to know you're important to him."

For our final class meeting, the day before school let out for the year, no assignment was due. It was my turn, I said, to give an oral report. I'd done my best to transform the class—to personalize it, and democratize it also—and it seemed only fair that I do the same work my students had done.

"You never did the same work before," one student said. "I'd have liked to make *you* memorize the Gettysburg Address and the names of all the secretaries of state."

"I'd have liked to make you take one of our tests," another student said.

This semester had been about change, I told them, and this was another change I'd instituted.

I spoke about the history of adoption. Originally, I explained, closed adoption was the rule. Hospital records were sealed, and the privacy of the birth mother was guaranteed. But in some states the laws were changing. Open adoption was becoming more common. Many children knew their birth parents and were establishing relationships with them.

I placed adoption in context: *Roe v. Wade* and the abortion struggle; delayed childbirth, surrogate motherhood, and the impoverished state of foster care; the children's rights and fatherhood movements, including court cases in which children sued their parents for divorce and fathers returned to claim their biological offspring.

My students weren't interested in this discussion. They preferred to hear me talk about myself, even if I didn't mention my sex life.

I gave them a brief personal history, outlining the Jewish laws my family observed. I sketched a replica on the blackboard of the map my father had drawn me of his ancestral homeland in White Russia. I'd known that I was adopted, but I'd believed I'd come from White Russia too. I'd seen myself as a long-lost cousin.

But then, I told my students, I found out I wasn't born Jewish.

"Were you baptized?" one student asked.

"No. My parents converted me and raised me as a Jew."

"But did your birth mother baptize you before she gave you up?"

"I don't think so."

"If you were baptized," the student said, "then you're Christian."

"Christianity is about belief," I said. "Judaism is essentialist."

"What does that mean?" a student asked.

"It means it's about essences. Either you're Jewish or you're not. It doesn't have anything to do with belief."

"It's a culture," another student said.

"Right. But it's also a religion."

"It's a race," said another.

"Not exactly."

"For Hitler's purposes," the last student said, "you were Jewish if any of your grandparents were. They killed you no matter what you believed."

"That's true," I said.

"I'm half Jewish," said a girl whose mother was Irish and whose father was a Hungarian Jew. I wondered if she knew the rabbis wouldn't agree with her. According to them, you were Jewish or you weren't. If fate had reversed itself—if her father had been Irish and her mother a Hungarian Jew—then she would have been welcomed in any synagogue in the world. How could that possibly have made sense to her? It didn't make sense even to me.

Paul, the adopted student, raised his hand. "I don't think your birth mother had the right to find you."

"Why not?"

"She violated your privacy."

I disagreed, I told him. It had been up to me whether to meet my birth mother. Besides, I was happy she found me.

"She had no way of knowing that. She gave you up. She has to live with the consequences."

"She's lived with the consequences and so have I."

"I think there should be a law," Paul said, "to prevent birth parents from tracking their kids down."

The next day, when school let out for the year, I drove across the Bay Bridge to Susan's apartment. She'd invited me for tea, to celebrate the end of the school year. I'd never been in her apartment before, and I felt like someone whose blindfold has been removed.

I was surprised by how well furnished the place was. Susan had come to San Francisco without plans to stay, yet her apartment looked like a real home. In the living room, where we sat, were a paisley sofa, a wicker rocking chair, a coffee table, a leather lounge chair, and a TV set. A rug was spread across the floor. On the wall above the fireplace hung a ceramic mask.

Susan went into the kitchen and brought back cups, saucers, and a pot of tea. The cups were white, with tea stains on the inside that looked like part of the pattern. Had these cups come with her from Indiana?

"How long are you planning to stay here?" I asked.

"I don't have any plans," she said coolly.

"You must. You said you've rented this apartment month to month, but look at all the furniture you have here. Did it come with the apartment? Is it yours? This doesn't feel like the home of someone only visiting."

"I may not be only visiting. I just don't know. Once I met you, I bought furniture and other things. I had my husband send some dishes from home."

"Who is your husband, anyway? You've hardly said anything about him."

"I told you who he is. He works in a bank. He was Scottie's father. We're having some trouble right now. That's all I feel like saying."

"Do you want to work things out?"

"If we can. But it's not always that easy."

"What's his name?"

"Ben—"

"I'm curious."

"All right. His name is Frank. But I don't see why it matters."

"It matters because he's your husband. And because you're my birth mother, and I'm curious about you."

"But you have to respect my privacy."

"What about *my* privacy? I spoke about you in class yesterday and one student said you didn't have the right to track me down."

"Did you agree?"

"No. But he has a point. At the very least, it's hypocritical for you to lecture me about privacy." I fingered the chipped edge of my teacup. "What about my birth father? You've told me next to nothing about him. And here I am in your apartment for the first time, and it looks like you've been living here for ages. You come bursting into my life, demanding that you meet people, but when it comes to you, you say nothing."

"Look," she said, "what happened with your birth father took place a long time ago. When I got pregnant, he disappeared. I don't have very good memories of him. Why should I help you find him?"

"Find him?"

"Isn't that why you want to know who he is?"

It wasn't, I told her. She was more than enough for me to handle.

"I just want to know a little bit about him. It's reasonable for me to be curious, don't you think?"

"Maybe it is. And I might tell you more about him sometime. But I don't feel like talking about it right now." She flipped over a magazine that had been lying facedown on the coffee table. It was a copy of *The American Spectator.*

"Do you read that?" Was Susan a Republican? I thought of my mother, a member of NOW and the ACLU, who used to have nightmares about Barry Goldwater chasing her through alleys in the middle of the night.

"Sometimes. My husband gave me a subscription. He wants me to learn more about politics. But I'm not interested."

She pointed to a framed photo on the table. "That's Scottie." He had a wide-set, open face, and green eyes, the color of Susan's, and light brown hair in a crew cut. On his chin was a birthmark. He was standing in front of a gray Oldsmobile, flashing a peace sign at the camera.

"I took that picture," Susan said. "You can see my thumb in the corner."

I touched my finger to the glass.

"It was a Sunday," she said. "We'd gone to church that morning. He died a week later, five days short of his twenty-first birthday. He was driving that car in the picture. The day he died, if I'd held him back for breakfast, if I'd kissed him good-bye, if I'd asked him one simple question—all I needed was a second's delay, and everything would have been different.

"He was on furlough from the Navy at the time. The other driver was killed too. He was the same age as Scottie. I wanted to know whose fault it was, but the wreck was so big the police couldn't be sure. I wanted it to be someone's fault, even if it had to be Scottie's. I can still see the hospital clearly. The other boy's mother was there too. We'd already been told that everything was over. I didn't know what to do, so I just fed all my change into the candy machine, even though I wasn't hungry."

Susan was smiling at Scottie's picture, almost as if she expected him to smile back. I thought of parents whose children lay in comas, who spent hours every day talking to them, thinking that if only they tried a little harder they would get a response.

"He's handsome," I told her.

"He looks a little like you."

"You're right," I said, although I didn't think he did.

She led me into her bedroom. Being there made me uncomfortable; I had to resist the urge to look around. On her desk, right in front of me, sat a stray earring. It was silver and shaped like Saturn, each of its rings a shade lighter than the next, moving out from the center.

"Did you do that?" I asked.

Susan nodded.

"When did you start to make earrings?"

"In eleventh grade."

"The year you got pregnant . . ."

"Right."

"Did I derail you?"

"You?"

"You know. The pregnancy. I have this idea that you were going places and I came along and screwed things up. Maybe you could have had your own line of jewelry. Then you wouldn't be selling your earrings in just a few stores."

"I wouldn't have wanted my own line of jewelry. It would have been too much work."

I asked her whether she was religious. I was trying to distract myself while, from the corner of my eye, I could see her unmade bed, and on it an unfolded pink nightgown.

She told me she was.

"What denomination are you?" I wondered how she'd feel if she knew that Jonathan used to pretend that he was crucified while I hit tennis balls against Riverside Church.

"Catholic." She reached inside her blouse and pulled out a gold cross so tiny it looked like a sliver of metal.

"Do you wear that all the time?"

"Except for the day I met you. I didn't want to make you uncomfortable."

"Did you baptize me?" I asked.

"Of course not. I was giving you up. I couldn't make decisions about how you'd be raised."

"You could have tried to place me with a Catholic family."

"It didn't matter to me. I just wanted you to have parents who loved you."

"You found them," I said. "I promise you that."

She looked as if she were going to cry.

The sun was setting on the Mission, dispersing across the rooftops. "I'm glad you sent me a Mother's Day card," she said. She rested her hand on the window ledge. Her veins caught the light of the sunset.

"It was nothing."

"You didn't have to do it. It meant a lot to me."

The phone rang in the kitchen, and Susan went to pick it up. I was alone. I heard the muffled sound of her voice down the hall. I stood quietly, allowing myself to look around the room for the first time. Susan's closet was ajar. I opened it the rest of the way. A gray silk scarf hung from a peg. I raised it to my nose to see if I could smell her, but I couldn't detect any scent. I closed the closet door and stood still awhile. Then, quietly, carefully, I opened drawer after drawer of her bureau, finding T-shirts in piles, blue jeans, slacks, towels, sheets, and a few light sweaters. In the top drawer were underpants and bras. The sight of them shocked me. Did I think she didn't wear any underpants? I shut the drawer firmly. Reflexively, I opened it again. Different colors. Black, white, red, some stripes and patterns. Cotton, silk, lace. I reached out to touch them. I raised a pair to my face, feeling the fabric against me. I quickly put it back and shut the drawer tight. A sick feeling overcame me.

I sat down on her bed, then got up and went to her desk. Papers were spread across it. An Indiana University mug held pens, pencils, and paper clips. An envelope lay beneath a roll of Scotch tape. I picked it up and read the return address. Indianapolis, Indiana. I took out the card and read it.

Dear Susan,

I'm sending you another check. I hope you're doing all right. We miss you here—everyone does, but especially me.

I saw Kate at the supermarket the other day. She asked about you. Your friends think this is strange, you going all the way across the country to see your "son." He could visit you here if he wanted. Believe me, he has his own life. I'm the one who needs you. Maybe I've been a bit remote recently, especially since Scottie died. But I'm willing to work on things.

I'm being patient with you, but really, how much longer can you expect me to be patient? I see our friends around town. I try hard to portray this in the best possible light, but it's difficult. Everyone thinks you've flipped. They say you've had some sort of breakdown. I tell them you haven't, but sometimes I'm not sure.

Remember that I'm thinking about you. If you need more money, let me know. The whole state of Indiana misses you.

Love,
Frank

I heard Susan's footsteps coming down the hall. I shoved the card and the envelope into my front pants pocket and swung around to face her. The edge of the envelope pressed against my belt.

She'd drawn me into her life, and there I was, rifling through her underwear drawer, reading her mail. I was a snoop, a voyeur. I wanted more than anything to leave her apartment, but that would have raised her suspicions.

"What's wrong?"

"Nothing." But everything was wrong. We both were pathetic. What was I doing in her apartment? Frank was right (Frank? I acted like I knew him). Susan had no business being in San Francisco. I didn't care how many earrings she'd sold. She'd come here to see me; we both knew that. "Look at us," I said. "What are we doing here?"

"I don't know what you're talking about."

"Why are you pretending you live here?" I was yelling now. I hated her—hated her wide-eyed obtuseness, hated what she'd done to me. "If it weren't for you, I'd be getting on with my life."

"That's ridiculous."

I took a step closer to her. "You gave me up when I was barely two months old. Do you think that doesn't have consequences?"

"Let me tell you something. Giving you up wasn't easy. But it was the best thing that ever happened to you."

"You weren't doing me any favors."

"I certainly was. Your life would have been a dead end if I'd kept you. We'd have been on welfare. You went to Yale, in case you forgot. Do you know how many people would love to be in your shoes?"

"Don't talk to me about Yale. I've heard it all before. I should appreciate my opportunities."

"Well, you should. Do you think Scottie was able to even think about Yale?"

"What does Scottie have to do with this?"

"He has everything to do with it. He was my son. Do you think he joined the Navy because he liked ships, or because he wanted to go to war? Not a chance. It was simply a way to get ahead. He was dealing with reality."

"Who says he was any less happy than I am?"

"I'm not talking about happy. I just wish you'd stop feeling sorry for yourself."

"You're one to talk." She'd come to town, I reminded her, with her sob story. Her son had died, she'd separated from her husband, she cried every year on my birthday. Did I really have a choice whether to meet her?

"Of course you did. I never asked for your pity."

"Not directly. But everything about you demands pity."

At home I felt one thing only—the need to make amends. I should have left matters as they were. Susan probably wouldn't have noticed anything missing, and she never would have suspected me. But I couldn't accept what I'd done. So I sent her husband a letter.

Dear Mr. Green,

You may not recognize my name, but I'm your wife's son—the one she gave birth to in high school. I want you to know she's doing all right and talks about you all the time. I was at her apartment recently, and she was reading a copy of *The American Spectator*. She appreciates the subscription you gave her. She enjoys the magazine. The separation is hard for her. I'm confident the two of you will work things out.

Best wishes,
Ben Suskind

I was surprised, now that Tara had left for camp, that I missed her as much as I did. The apartment felt emptier than I'd expected. She'd be gone until the end of August.

The day she left, Jenny and I took her to the bus stop. As the bus pulled out of sight, there were tears in Jenny's eyes; then I realized there were tears in mine too.

That night I said, "Privacy's not what it's cracked up to be, is it?"

"It sure isn't." We were in the den, watching a video. We'd ordered in pizza, the remains of which were in the box; we were lying half naked on the floor. Yet our minds were on Tara.

"This is the longest I'll have gone without seeing her," Jenny said.

"I was thinking about that."

"In seven years she'll be leaving for college. That's less than three thousand days away."

The first week Tara was gone, Jenny and I would find ourselves in her bedroom, talking, doing a crossword puzzle, sometimes reading a novel to each other. It felt as if we were communing with her. We had another sabbath dinner the first Friday night she was away, but it didn't feel the same without her. I kept looking at her empty seat as if I expected to find her there.

At the beginning of the second week, we got a postcard from her.

Dear Mom and Ben,

Please send peanut butter. Camp food sucks. Amy and I have been hunting for berries.

Love,
Tara

P.S. The whole bunk listens to Oasis. Ugh.

"She's happy!" Jenny said. "She's doing well."

"Who's Amy?"

"I don't know. A bunkmate. Someone who likes berries."

We started to adjust to our new freedom. We ate out a little more often. We let the dishes pile up in the sink. We got stoned one night with some pot a friend of Jenny's had given her; we hadn't gotten stoned in almost a year.

Jenny nuzzled against me. "I like having you to myself."

Two weeks after Tara left, Jenny enrolled in a photography course at the San Francisco Art Institute. She was excited about the class. She wanted to spend the summer taking photographs and experimenting in the darkroom.

But her work got busier. Her rape client's semen sample came back a match, and this led Jenny to believe it was a closed case; her client should plea-bargain, she thought.

Her client changed his story, however. Originally he'd said he hadn't been at the scene of the crime. Now he admitted that he'd had sex with the accuser, but said the sex was consensual. Jenny was suspicious. Her client and the accuser were from such different backgrounds they were unlikely to have spent time together. Under questioning, though, the accuser admitted having been to the bar that Jenny's client had named. Still, the accuser said, she'd never met him, never even seen him until he raped her that night.

Jenny was convinced that her client was lying; he'd lied once already, after all. In rape cases like this one, the defense often tried to smear the accuser's sexual reputation. Jenny owed her client the best defense possible, but she didn't think she could employ such tactics.

"I'm being a bad lawyer," she told me.

"Come on, Jen. You're the best lawyer I know."

"You live with me. You're biased."

"I'm not biased. I just recognize something good when I see it."

Jenny told her client that she thought she could get him a reduced sentence. She *did* think that, but mostly she just wanted to get rid of the case.

"It will be good to go away," I said. I was taking her on a vacation, as I'd promised. We would drive down the coast to Big Sur and spend a long weekend there. "You'll have a chance to get your mind off things."

"Maybe we should just skip going away."

"Jen. Come on."

"You're right. I want to go. And you've been planning this."

On the way to Big Sur, Jenny sat next to me while I drove. Our camping gear was in back. We'd spend one night camping and two nights at a bed-and-breakfast. We stopped for lunch at Half Moon Bay, then got back into the car. Jenny took photos of me as we drove.

"You're going to end up with a lot of pictures of my right ear."

"I'm experimenting." She leaned back in her seat and closed her eyes. "Sometimes I wish I were disgustingly rich. I could be one of those ladies who have tea all the time. I'd sit in a Viennese salon and fan myself."

"You'd be bored stiff as a tea lady."

"It would be nice not to have to go to court. I could just take pictures."

"But you love being a PD."

"I'm burning out. With photography, the worst thing you can do is take bad pictures. You're not ruining anyone's life."

"Or saving anyone's either."

Jenny shrugged. "Sometimes I just need to get away."

"That's why we're on vacation."

We bought salmon steaks and grilled them at our campsite. We went to bed early and made love in our tent on top of our sleeping bags, then lay quietly, staring at the stars through the mesh of our tent.

"Big Sur," Jenny said, pressing her face to my chest. "I can hear the bears growl." When I'd hiked the Appalachian Trail I'd come across a bear cub. The story had gotten embellished over time, so that now it was a grizzly and I'd actually struggled with it. It had become a joke between Jenny and me.

The next morning we moved to the bed-and-breakfast, where our room was large and comfortable, with a complimentary bottle of champagne in the refrigerator. Out back was a Jacuzzi. Downstairs, twenties and thirties show tunes played on the jukebox.

Monday, when we drove home, was my birthday. On our way back, Jenny took a turn before Half Moon Bay, saying she had a surprise for me. She drove me to a bowling alley, which had my name and a happy-birthday greeting on the marquee.

Balloons were taped to the chairs behind our lane. Jenny had arranged to have seventies music playing on the speakers. A waiter and a waitress came to take our orders. They were dressed as Elton John and Kiki Dee.

"Happy birthday." Jenny kissed me. "We can eat Hostess cupcakes and listen to the Bee Gees and Andy Gibb." She took a picture of me with the waiter and the waitress.

A Donna Summer song was playing. "Dance with me," Jenny said. She rested her left hand on my hip; she cupped her right hand behind my neck and led me down the lane toward the pins, then danced me slowly back.

She uncorked the champagne, which we'd saved from our room at the bed-and-breakfast. I bowled a few frames while Jenny danced to "The Hustle."

"What do you think would have happened if we'd met in the seventies?"

"We probably would have pulled each other's hair," Jenny said.

"I mean the late seventies. When we were teenagers. Do you think we would have liked each other?"

"I doubt it. I was a wild teenager. I didn't go out with boys like you."

"I'd have liked you," I told her.

Jenny shook her head. "It's good we didn't meet until now."

I'd thought our vacation would rejuvenate Jenny, but after a day back at work, she was tense again. Her rape suspect hadn't gone away, and she'd gotten a new load of cases. Tara had been at camp for a month. We'd received only two letters since her first card, and she'd asked us not to come up for visiting day. She wanted to be on her own the whole summer. She'd see us when she got back.

"It's a sign she's happy," I told Jenny. "No news is good news."

But Jenny clearly missed her.

Soon after we returned from our trip, Jenny was commissioned by *The San Francisco Bay Guardian* to do a photo essay on Polk Gulch, where teenage boys sold sex to men and where there had been a series of unsolved murders. Jenny's photography teacher had recommended her to the editor.

At first, Jenny hesitated. "The summer's supposed to be relaxing, and I'm spreading myself too thin." She needed to concentrate on her work. In a month, we'd be going to New York for my parents' annual Labor Day party and to surprise my father on his seventy-fifth birthday. That too would break up her routine.

She was flattered, though, that her teacher had recommended her, and she wanted the chance to publish her photos. So she took the assignment.

I was nervous. Polk Gulch was a seedy, dangerous place. Jenny would spend nights walking the streets, cruising with her camera around her neck, cozying up to the Johns by the dim light of a bar.

The first two nights I drove her there and waited nearby until she was done shooting. But the next night she insisted on going alone. "It's my work," she said. "I can't be distracted."

I was afraid something would happen to her.

"Don't worry," Jenny said, and she squeezed my hand. "I'll be all right."

Yet I had to wonder about her judgment. She had married Steve while still in college—married him on a whim, it seemed to me, going to City Hall one afternoon accompanied by a witness they'd met on BART. She'd given birth to Tara a year later, not knowing what she would do when she left school or how she would support her. From the start, she said, she'd had no idea if the marriage would work. Steve walked out when Tara was still an infant, carrying his belongings on the back of his motorcycle. He drove that motorcycle wherever he went, drove it on the freeways without a helmet—a sure sign that he was irresponsible and that the marriage was doomed from the start.

"Lots of people drive motorcycles," Jenny said to me once.

"I know. James Dean drove a motorcycle. Look what happened to him."

"James Dean died in a car crash."

"So what? If it hadn't been one thing it would have been another."

Jenny had told me she'd gone hang-gliding in college. She was older now, but she still took risks. And I still worried about her.

Meanwhile, I had time on my hands. I'd been sleeping late, then going to play basketball in playgrounds around the city. I'd been rereading Dickens. I'd taken up jogging to get in better shape.

My sloth bothered Jenny. She didn't like that I was lounging around while she was working doubly hard.

I volunteered to take on extra household duties. I made sure to do the laundry and prepare dinner. I cleaned the apartment and paid the bills. But I still had lots of free time. And Jenny wasn't pleased.

"You should do something," she said.

"I *am* doing something. I'm playing basketball and reading Dickens."

"I mean really do something. Something constructive."

"Jen, you're the one who wanted to be a tea lady. So I'm being a tea lady for both of us."

She wasn't amused.

During the second week of August, my boss called to tell me that the chair of the history department had had a heart attack and would have to retire. The school was looking for a replacement—a younger teacher to take a three-year renewable term—and he wanted to know if I was interested. I said I'd get back to him, but I was only stalling before I said no. I didn't want to seem rash or ungrateful. The offer was last-minute; I'd have to spend the next month working on the curriculum. Besides, I didn't want to commit to a three-year term.

This made Jenny angry.

"What difference does it make if I'm chair of the department?"

"It makes no difference. I just hate your reasons for not doing it."

"Like what?"

"Like the fact that you don't want to work this summer."

"Well, I don't."

"Or the fact that you won't commit to a three-year term."

"What's wrong with that? I'm not even sure I want to be teaching in three years."

"What do you want to be doing in three years?"

"That's the point. I don't know."

"What *do* you know?"

"Stop it. I know plenty of things. Don't make me out to be more aimless than I am."

"You're not aimless. You're conflicted."

"Stop analyzing me."

"You couldn't commit to a three-day term, let alone a three-year term."

I glared at her.

"All right. Let's forget about this."

"Yes," I said. "Let's."

But Jenny didn't forget about it. Every issue bled into others; everything had to do with our relationship. When we came back from Big Sur, I'd seen an advertisement for an adoptees' support group and decided to join. The group met once a week for dinner at members' houses. Almost immediately, I volunteered to host.

This too upset Jenny. Fifteen minutes before the other members arrived, she left the apartment for the evening. "I'm out of here," she said.

When she came home, she asked me about our get-together and whether I was enjoying my secret life.

"I don't have a secret life."

"Once a week you meet a bunch of strangers and confess to each other."

"They're not strangers and nobody confesses. You have no idea what it's like."

"What's it like, then? It sounds like the Rotary Club, or some men's group where you read Robert Bly and get up in the middle of the night and paint each other's houses."

"Come on, Jen. It's just a bunch of us getting together. We talk about what it's like to be adopted."

"You've got adoption on the brain."

"That's not true."

"The problem is you're rooted in the past, and therefore the two of us are in limbo." Susan had given me up thirty-one years ago, she said, and I pretended it had just happened. But it hadn't just happened. The past was the past and now was now; we needed to decide where our relationship was going.

"Going?" I said. "We live together. We wake up in the morning in the same bed. We share our secrets. Where does a relationship need to go?"

"We live together now. But will we live together next month, or next year?"

"I hope so."

"And will we get married? I'm thirty-two years old, Ben, and I might want to have another child. Do you want children? We've been going out for two and a half years, and I realized the other day I had no idea if you do. There are all these things we never talk about."

She was right. We rarely talked about the future. It was mostly my fault.

"You've met Susan," she said. "Don't you think that's enough?"

"You're the one who encouraged me to meet her."

"I know I did. But I was hoping it would help you move on. Now you know where you come from. Is it that I'm not Jewish?"

"That's part of it." But if I wasn't willing to marry a non-Jew, what was I doing living with Jenny, living with her as if we were in fact married, quietly assuming we had a future?

"Well, that's not going to change. I won't be Jewish next year or the year after that. I'm sorry, Ben. There's nothing I can do about it."

"I know."

"I love you, but we can't pretend we're twenty. We need to make plans, together or apart."

"We will," I said. "I promise."

But things stayed tense between Jenny and me. She'd get angry over insignificant matters—a pair of mismatched socks I accidentally placed in her drawer; the music on too loud while she was preparing for work; my showing up five minutes late to meet her for dinner.

"I'm sorry," she finally said. "I'm being unfair."

"It's all right."

"Tara will be home in a week, and things will settle down."

I was counting on that. I thought of Tara as some kind of savior, as a calming influence at the very least.

Then one morning I got a call from Jonathan. He sounded terrible, his voice so hoarse I almost didn't recognize it.

"Are you all right?"

"I've got a fever," he croaked.

"Where's Sandy?"

"In New Mexico. Visiting his parents. I can't think straight."

When I got to Jonathan's, I was carrying Tylenol, Pepto-Bismol, two cans of Cherry Coke, a hot-water bottle, some throat lozenges, and a jar of Vicks VapoRub. I didn't know what all of his symptoms were, so I'd brought everything I could find.

He'd left the door to the house unlocked. He was lying in bed, half asleep.

"You look terrible." I placed my hand on his forehead. He had a high fever.

"I've never been this sick. I'm going to die."

"You're not going to die." But I was scared. This was how AIDS started. You got colds. You became weaker. Jonathan looked worn-out and pale; he was congested. Crumpled wads of tissue dotted the floor. He'd been too sick to throw them out. He had the flu. Who got the flu in August?

I didn't know much about AIDS, but I found myself looking for symptoms. He had no lesions on his body. He was thin, but he'd always been thin. I couldn't ask him if he was HIV-positive. He hadn't been willing to discuss it before, and I was too scared to raise it now.

I gave him a glass of Cherry Coke.

"Maybe I have the mumps," he said.

"You don't have the mumps."

"That's right. I had them already."

"You never had them."

"That's what I get for pretending."

Good. He still had his sense of humor. "You'll be all right."

"I need to throw up." He pulled himself out of bed and found his way to the bathroom.

I spent the afternoon with him as he drifted in and out of sleep, then made him toast and tea for dinner. I turned the radio on to a classical station in the hope that the music would soothe him. I went home and packed a bag, telling Jenny I would spend the night with him. I slept on the couch in his living room.

The next morning, he seemed a little better. His temperature had gone down, and he was able to walk around a bit. But when he stood for too long he became woozy and nauseated and had to get back into bed.

He called in sick to work. I spent the morning with him watching television, playing channel-changer. "Next," he said when he got bored, and I switched to another talk show, another soap opera, another news program.

I left around noon, telling him I'd be back in a few hours, and went to the nearest branch of the public library, where I sat in the reference section and read through medical encyclopedias. I found entire sections on AIDS. There were too many opportunistic infections to count. Some I'd heard of, many I hadn't. Tuberculosis. Kaposi's sarcoma. Meningitis. Non-Hodgkin's lymphoma. Toxoplasmosis. Thrush. Lymphadenopathy. Cytomegalovirus. Each infection had its own arcane language, which took me to the medical dictionary, which in turn introduced me to more words I didn't know. Two hours at the library, and I'd come across a greater number of painful ways to die than I'd imagined possible.

In the evening, Jonathan's fever broke. I spent the night at home. When I called him the next morning he sounded back to normal. He was getting ready to go to the office.

But I was still shaken. Though he was better now, this might have been the beginning of something much worse.

That day, I wandered through the Castro, staring at the men I passed. Some were obviously sick. A few were sallow and skeletal; others were covered with purple lesions. Several men walked with canes. One was led by a Seeing Eye dog. Others looked healthy, but you never knew. Fifty percent was the figure I'd heard. I stared at everyone, trying to find a common denominator among the men I saw.

I strolled along Market Street, then up Castro to Twenty-fourth, then east to Noe, then back to Market. I may as well have been doing laps. All the while I worried about Jonathan, and imagined gruesome things that could happen to him.

I called him at work to see how he was feeling.

"I'm fine," he said. "My fever's gone."

"Are you sure?"

He told me he was.

I called him again the next afternoon, from a pay phone near the basketball court where I was playing.

"Are you all right?" I asked.

"Why wouldn't I be?"

"You were sick."

"That was days ago, Ben. I'm fine. I told you. You sound like a Jewish mother."

"I'm just worried about you."

"Well, don't be."

When I got home that afternoon, a letter was waiting for me.

Dear Mr. Suskind,

I received your letter. I wasn't planning to respond to it, but suffise it to say, I've changed my mind. I'm in touch with Susan. She's still my wife. I know how she's doing. I'd prefer it if you'd mind your own business. Don't patronize me. Susan's out there to see you, and if your feeling guilty about it, keep it to yourself. What's happening in my marriage is my business—mine and Susan's. I'm not interested in your counseling. I try to have better manners than this, and I'm not usually so abrupt with strangers. But I want to make myself perfectly clear.

Sincerely,
Frank Green

My first thought was, Bad spelling and grammar. *Suffice* was with a *c*. *You're feeling*, not *your feeling*. No wonder Susan was spending time with me. I had good spelling and grammar, and Frank didn't.

My second thought was, Oh shit. I'd gotten Frank angry, as I should have expected. Had he told Susan about my letter? Maybe she was waiting for me to confess. That was almost worse—not knowing, being dangled.

I called her up to see if she'd say anything.

"How are things with your husband?" I asked.

"About what you'd expect."

But that was the problem. I didn't know what to expect. That was how everything went with Susan. It was one day this, another day that.

"I wouldn't know what to expect," I said.

"Well, I'm here and he's there. That should say something."

Maybe he hadn't told her.

When Tara came home, I was relieved. I hugged her in the doorway to our apartment. "I missed you," I said. "I really did."

"You act like I was kidnapped or something." Tara told us about Amy, her new best friend, who was born in New York City. Amy and Tara had given each other crew cuts. "I'm moving to New York," Tara said. She gave Jenny a list of new dietary restrictions, although it wasn't clear what unified them. She said she no longer ate processed food. She told Jenny that she wanted to go to boarding school on the East Coast, that it was time for her to live on her own, the way she had in the wilderness at camp.

"Boarding school isn't in the wilderness," Jenny said. "It's in boring towns in Massachusetts where the headmaster makes sure you're properly dressed and you have to do a lot of homework. Besides, it's expensive and you're too young to go."

But Tara was insistent. "I'll pay for it," she said. "I'll start baby-sitting."

"You'll have to baby-sit a few hundred years in order to pay for boarding school."

"I got a new hole in my ear."

Jenny frowned. "I noticed. I hope you used a sterilized needle."

"I did it with a fork."

"You did not."

"I'm going to school on the East Coast because I can't stand California."

"What's wrong with California?" I asked.

"It's boring."

I ran my hand through the fuzz on her head. "I, for one, like California."

"That's easy for you to say. You got to grow up in New York."

"And you get to grow up in San Francisco, where the ocean is only a few miles away and you can play outdoors all year."

"I like cold weather."

"Well, Ben and I have good news for you," Jenny said. We told Tara about our plans for a trip to New York to surprise my father for his birthday.

On a Friday morning, Jenny, Tara, and I flew to New York. Sandy and Jonathan would come later that afternoon, after they were done with work.

"You and I are flying separately," Jonathan joked, "so that if one of us gets killed, the other will be around to take care of Mom and Dad."

Someday we *would* have to take care of them. My father was healthy, but he'd started to slow down. My previous visit to New York, I'd found myself testing him, quickening my gait as we walked together, hoping that he could keep up with me.

I sat on the plane between Jenny and Tara, reading a copy of *Time* magazine. A movie was playing—something with Arnold Schwarzenegger or Jean-Claude Van Damme—but I hadn't rented the headphones. I tried to read the actors' lips.

I'd ordered a kosher meal. I always did this when I flew, for sentimental reasons more than anything else. When I was a child, I liked getting the kosher meal in its unperforated wrapping, my name stamped on the foil as if the food had been mailed to me directly from God.

We landed at Kennedy late that afternoon. My parents wouldn't be there; they didn't know we were coming. Even so, as we walked toward the baggage claim area, I scanned the names on the cardboard signs.

We reached the apartment at seven. "Happy Labor Day," I said when my parents opened the door. "Happy birthday, Dad."

"Oh my God," my mother said.

We all hugged one another. Then we huddled in a big hug. My parents were thrilled to see the three of us—even Jenny, it seemed.

"What are you doing here?" my father asked.

"It's your birthday, Dad. I'll never again have a father who turns seventy-five."

He smiled. "I hope you'll be here on my hundred and twentieth." That's what he was entitled to hope for. Jews prayed to live as long as Moses.

"We're a little short on food," my mother said, "but we'll manage."

Tara emptied her pockets of a dozen packets of peanuts she'd stolen from the plane.

My mother touched her hand. "You got a haircut, hon."

"And another hole in my ear."

My father said the kiddush. He and I sang the sabbath songs, everyone else humming with us. The room was warm, the candles flickered, and I kicked off my shoes and rested my feet on the carpet, feeling Jenny's toes pressed against mine.

"I'm glad you're all here," my mother said.

"We are too," said Jenny.

My parents' magazines sat next to the grand piano. Years of issues were accumulated there. Friday night at midnight, when the lamps went off, my father would press his *New York Review of Books* against the window, hoping to read another paragraph in the light from the streetlamps.

At eleven there was a knock on the door. My mother looked startled when she opened it. Jonathan and Sandy were standing there, tired smiles on their faces.

"I don't believe it." My mother turned to me. "Did you know about this?"

"No." I laughed.

"Of course he knew, Mom." Jonathan walked over and kissed her. He kissed my father too.

We all sat in the living room. "You boys," said my mother, shaking her head. I thought I could see tears in my parents' eyes.

Around midnight my father went to bed. My mother removed five sets of towels from the linen closet. She handed a set each to Jenny, me, and Tara and placed the other sets on Jonathan's bed along with a second pillow.

"You're letting us sleep together?" Jonathan asked. Sandy had visited the apartment only twice, and both times they'd slept in separate rooms.

"You're adults," my mother said, "and if Jenny and Ben are going to sleep together, it's only fair to be consistent. And Dad's gone to sleep, so he doesn't need to know." She fluffed up the pillows on Jonathan's bed and patted down the blankets. "Besides, where else am I going to put you guys?"

That night in bed I asked Jenny, "Do you think Jonathan has AIDS?"

"What?" She sat up. "Where did you get that idea?"

"The thought must have occurred to you."

"I just always assumed—"

"When he got sick a couple of weeks ago—he was really sick, Jen, you should have seen him—I couldn't stop thinking about it. I didn't want to say anything to you then. I was too scared."

"But he's fine now."

"He *seems* fine. But who gets the flu in August?"

"He and Sandy are monogamous, aren't they?"

"I assume so. But there's the time they broke up after college, and whoever else they slept with before they started going out."

"You could ask him if he's positive. He's your brother, you know."

"I can't. I tried in college, but he wouldn't talk about it. And what if he's positive? I'd kill myself."

"No you wouldn't."

She was right. But it was more than just a figure of speech. It wasn't simply that I couldn't imagine his dying. I couldn't fathom living without him. Even now that we were older and much had changed between us, he was the closest approximation to me in the world. We shared something deeper than genes.

"He looks healthy, don't you think?"

"Magic Johnson looks healthy too," I said.

The next day, Saturday, my father went to services and my mother slept in, and the rest of us ate breakfast at a diner on Columbus Avenue, where we sat and read the paper. Then Sandy and Jonathan went to the Metropolitan Museum, while Jenny, Tara, and I took the subway down to Greenwich Village. Amy had told Tara about the Village, and Tara had insisted we go there.

"That's where I'm going to live when I grow up," Tara said. "When I finally escape California."

"The East Village or the West Village?" I asked.

"Who cares? The whole thing's the Village." She rolled her eyes at me, as if I were the one in New York for the first time and my ignorance of the Village were too embarrassing to countenance.

We had lunch on Bleecker Street, then wandered in and out of boutiques and used-clothing stores. Tara tried on a denim jacket she wanted Jenny to buy for her, but Jenny said it was too expensive.

We were going to take the subway uptown so I could show Jenny and Tara my old high school.

"We've spent less than an hour in the Village," Tara said.

"That's not true, hon," said Jenny. "We've spent close to three hours here, and there are other things to do in New York."

"Who wants to see Ben's high school anyway?"

"I do," Jenny said.

The school was on the Upper East Side. I hadn't been back in many years. Although it was Saturday and the doors were locked, I could make out the bank of elevators.

"That was my locker," I told Jenny. "Number three eighty-four."

Jenny pressed her nose against the glass.

"I still remember the smell. Sweaty gym clothes and chocolate-covered doughnuts. Jonathan and I stored Entenmann's in there."

"Where do the elevators go?" Jenny asked.

"To the classrooms."

"I can't believe you went here."

"Why not?"

"Who takes elevators to class? That's about as real as going to school in a spaceship."

"You probably hung out in treehouses after school."

"As a matter of fact, I did."

"That's a lot stranger than taking elevators to class. It sounds like *Little House on the Prairie*."

Jenny turned around. "Where's Tara?"

She was gone.

"Oh my God!" Jenny said.

We were standing between Fifth and Madison avenues. I ran toward Fifth and Jenny ran toward Madison, although it wasn't clear why either of us was running. We could have passed her in our haste.

I ran back and forth across the street. I must have looked like a madman. Out of breath, I asked several doormen whether they'd seen a girl walk by, or whether they'd noticed anything suspicious. They hadn't. I stopped a few strangers on the sidewalk, but no one seemed eager to help. I ran back toward Madison Avenue, where Jenny too was stopping strangers. She looked frantic.

I headed uptown while Jenny headed down. I stopped everyone I passed. I thought I spotted Tara's back inside a bakery, but the girl who turned around was Asian. I flagged down a policeman, but when I told him what had happened, he wasn't helpful. He assured me that Tara would show up soon.

I ran back to the corner where I'd separated from Jenny. She was standing there unsure of what to do. She had had no luck either.

Then we saw her. She walked out of a grocery store, eating an apple.

"Where the hell were you?" Jenny grabbed Tara by the arm. "You scared the shit out of me." I wasn't sure whether she meant to hug her or strangle her. I'd never seen her hit Tara before, but it occurred to me that she might do it right then.

"I was hungry." Tara spoke as casually as she would have if someone had asked her the time. "I wanted an apple."

"Give me that." Jenny grabbed the apple from Tara's hand, wheeled around, and threw it across Madison Avenue. It bounced against the curb.

"Come on, Jen," I said. "She's all right."

"You be quiet!" She'd thrown the apple so hard it could have hurt someone. It easily could have hit a passing car. Jenny grabbed Tara again by the arm.

"You're hurting me, Mom. Let go."

"Tell me what you thought you were doing, Tara. Do you know how scared I was?"

"I just went for a walk."

"This is New York. It's a dangerous city."

Tara gave her an insolent look. "You've been watching too much TV."

"I certainly haven't. This is life, not TV."

"If I want to take a walk, I can take a walk. I'm going to live here someday."

"You may or may not. But right now you're eleven years old, and you don't live in New York City. You live in San Francisco with Ben and me."

"It's your problem for not noticing that I left."

"My problem?"

"You should have seen the two of you—standing there staring at a bunch of elevators."

"That happens to be Ben's high school."

"Well, la-dee-da." Tara began to cry.

"What's wrong now?" Jenny asked.

"Forget it."

"Okay. I will."

"I'll tell you what's wrong," Tara said. "Everything. You've got your rape case and Ben's got his birth mother, and you're celebrating the sabbath like you're a Jew or something, Mom. No one even notices me."

"That's not true. Do you have any idea how much we missed you when you were at camp?"

"Well, I'm here now. Why are we in New York, anyway?"

"You love New York. We just went to Greenwich Village because you wanted to go there."

"We're not here for me. We're here for Ben's dad. So he's seventy-five years old. Who cares?"

"I do," Jenny said. "So does Ben. It wouldn't be the worst thing if you cared as well. When you get to be seventy-five, you might think it's a cause for celebrating."

On the bus ride home all three of us were quiet. Tara looked out the window, ignoring us. I held Jenny's hand and tried to comfort her.

She spoke to Tara. "I want to explain something to you. I'd have been glad to let you get an apple. But you can't walk off without telling me. It has nothing to do with how old you are. I wouldn't walk off without telling you either."

Tara kept staring out the window.

When we got home, I said nothing to my parents about what

had happened. Tara went into the bedroom where she was sleeping. When I closed the door behind us in my room, Jenny started to cry.

"I'm sorry," I said. "I really am."

"It's not your fault."

"I should have been paying better attention."

"*I* should have. I'm her mother." She lay facedown on my bed. "This is crazy, Ben. We shouldn't have come here."

"I had to come. It's my father's birthday."

"But I should have stayed home with Tara. She's starting school next week. Why am I shuttling her across the country?"

"Do you want to go home now?"

"I can't."

"I'll explain it to my parents. They'll understand."

"No," she said. "I'm all right."

After *havdala*, my parents took Jenny, Sandy, and Tara to the movies. Jonathan and I stayed at home and prepared a surprise album for my father.

We removed boxes from a storage closet and searched through them. We found a few photos of my father as a child. In one, he stood next to his brother Marvin, both of them holding a huge fish. You might have thought they had gone fishing and were showing off their catch, but they were actually standing on the Lower East Side; you could see the Hebrew lettering on the storefronts. My father looked timid. I couldn't believe this was the same person who'd brought me up, who walked confidently across the Columbia campus, who genuinely believed that if he didn't call attention to himself, if he said his prayers, ate well, and rode his stationary bicycle each day before work, he'd be teaching political science when he was a hundred.

Jonathan found my father's eighth-grade valedictory speech, dated June 14, 1933. He'd spoken about his faith in President Roosevelt and the commitment Jews should have to helping others, as embodied in the Torah and in Roosevelt's Hundred Days. He used words like "sanguine" and "munificence." I thought of the vocabulary book I'd given Jonathan and the hours we'd spent quizzing each other, until we knew so many words we simply chanted them. I imagined a competition—Uncle Marvin and my father versus Jonathan and me, all of us in eighth grade, seeing who had the best vocabulary.

"Do you think we used *sanguine* and *munificence* when we were in eighth grade?"

"Of course we did," Jonathan answered. "You got me that vocabulary book two years before. I bet we knew those words when we were eight."

"You think so?"

"We knew *obstreperous* when we were ten."

"Thanks to Dad," I said. He'd told us to stop being obstreperous. I couldn't imagine that. Who used words like *obstreperous* with a ten-year-old?

"It was thanks to our brains," Jonathan said. "Thanks to our Bill Bradley memories."

I found a Yankee scorecard from 1928. The Yankees had been playing the Boston Red Sox. Lou Gehrig hit a home run that day. In the boxes of the scorecard were Hebrew letters in my father's handwriting: *aleph* for a single, *bet* for a double—the secret code my father taught us when we watched the Mets at Shea Stadium.

We came across a letter from North Africa dated October 3, 1942. It was a love letter to a Gwen sent by a Theodore. My father must have written it for an army mate one night in the bunkers. I had no idea why the letter hadn't been sent and what it was doing in our apartment. I found another pile of letters, stashed in an old shoe box, written between my mother and father during their courtship. We started to read them but stopped; we were invading their privacy. I wondered what we'd do when they died, what we'd read and what we wouldn't, what we'd keep and what we'd throw out.

"Dear Francine," Jonathan said, holding up a piece of stationery and pretending to read a letter from my father to my mother. "Come see me in Paris. We'll eat baguettes by the banks of the Seine and sing French nursery songs at the Eiffel Tower." When we were toddlers, they'd played French nursery songs for us on the stereo. *Sur le pont d'Avignon l'on y danse tout en rond.* The summer after our freshman year of college, Jonathan and I had traveled to Europe, and made a special trip to Avignon to see the bridge we'd sung about.

I found a picture of my parents dated July 1962. My mother wore a yellow-and-white-striped tank top; my father was shirtless, burly, and dark. I thought of them as they'd once been, looking toward the horizon, the future.

"Do you think Mom's pregnant?" Jonathan asked. He pointed at the photograph.

"What do you mean?"

"You know. The miscarried baby."

I'd forgotten about that. I tried to determine whether they seemed lonely, this childless couple staring across the ocean, their faces clear and handsome.

I asked Jonathan where he thought those pictures were that he'd taken of me every month.

"They're probably in storage. In one of our closets, I'm sure."

"With our baseball cards."

"And our Wacky Packages. Remember them?"

I did. I also remembered subscribing to record clubs, receiving all those albums for a dollar, only we kept getting charged for new ones each month. They sent us John Denver and Barry Manilow. For a while we listened to Billy Joel. It wasn't until Bruce Springsteen, I reminded Jonathan, that our taste got better—Bruce Springsteen, whom our father called Bruce Springstine, some Jewish rock-'n'-roller from New Jersey.

"The things Dad didn't know," I said.

"He had no idea who Johnny Carson was."

"Or Rod Stewart."

"Or Elvis Presley."

"He knew Elvis," I said.

"All right. He knew Elvis."

Jonathan went to bed. The album was finished, and I was going to return the boxes to the storage closet. But I couldn't bring myself to put them away. I sat with them for a while longer on the floor.

I ran my hand across some photographs, just to touch them, really. I filed through old grade-school report cards. *Ben is becoming more assertive with his peers. He needs to work on his penmanship.*

I came across a sealed envelope, which I opened. Inside were several sheets of paper, and on the top page the words *State of Illinois.* This was a photocopy of a birth certificate, I realized, but it belonged to someone I didn't know—Michael Ivan Harris. It reminded me of the letter from Theodore to Gwen, all the odd items that were stored in this apartment.

Michael Ivan Harris had been born at Northwestern Memorial Hospital at eight twenty-three in the morning on December 21, 1964. Suddenly I realized what I was holding. Jonathan's birth certificate! He'd been born in Chicago and had a different name. Everything about him was in my hands: how much he'd weighed and how tall he'd been, and attached to the birth certificate were his adoption papers with the lawyers' signatures and the signatures of my parents, as well as the signatures of his birth parents, Alfred and Rebecca Harris. They had the same last name, so they must have been married. Harris. Was it a Jewish name? I got paranoid, sure that my parents would be home in a minute. They'd see me sitting with all those boxes and immediately know what I'd found.

Jonathan's door was shut. I could wake him up and tell him. But maybe I should wait until morning, or even until we got back to San Francisco. Who knew how he'd react with the family around?

He could fly to Chicago to meet his birth parents. I'd go with him if he wanted. I'd be there to guide him; I'd been through this already. As the months passed, everything would make sense. It wouldn't matter that he was gay, because we'd have this in common: meeting our birth mothers the same year.

I took his papers and hid them in my suitcase. The next day I'd make a copy of them. I'd return them to their envelope and place them back in the box. No one would know what I had done.

In the morning, I told everyone I was going to do some errands. I went to a Kinko's, where I made two sets of copies of Jonathan's papers. One set I folded and put in my pants pocket, and in case it got lost, I mailed the other set to myself in San Francisco.

On the way back to my parents' apartment, I imagined what would happen if I got mugged. I'd be left unconscious in the gutter, and the police would empty my pockets. They'd think I was Michael Ivan Harris. Then they'd find my wallet and notify my parents. I'd have a lot of explaining to do.

The next afternoon, at the Labor Day party, I chatted with my parents' friends and colleagues. My father's album was sitting in my bedroom, along with the gifts we'd gotten him for his birthday. We would give them to him after the guests had left.

I introduced Jenny to my parents' friends. She was doing better, but she still seemed tentative. She'd stare over the shoulder of the person she was talking to, looking for Tara.

Jonathan and Sandy were in the living room. I watched my

brother from various angles. Did he look different to me? Michael Ivan Harris from Chicago. I had to know why his parents had given him up. I felt offended for him—more offended than I'd felt for myself—at the idea of parents who didn't want him.

I tried to make sense of him as someone else: a kid named Michael, wandering through the halls of the Chicago Art Institute, eating deep-dish pizza, rooting for the White Sox—or worse, the Cubs—doing all the stereotypical Chicago things I could think of. Where would he be if he hadn't been adopted? At a Labor Day party in Chicago? Would he be a doctor? Would he be gay? Would he be a Jew?

But I kept all these questions to myself, kept everything to myself, as had become my habit. Perhaps I should have known then what I know now—that secrecy leads to trouble. I'd been so honest as a boy that one time, when the city bus I was on broke down, I walked the remaining mile and a half to school because the small print on the back of my bus pass said that I was allowed to use it only once going to school and once coming home. It amuses me what a stickler I was for the letter of the law, how unwilling I was to lie or cheat under any circumstances.

Did that boy understand something I've forgotten as an adult? The rabbis teach us that one sin begets another. Draw a fence around the Torah, they say, for if you even come close to disobeying the word of God, the next step is surely to disobey Him. As a boy I'd been honest to a fault. If I'd remained as scrupulous as an adult, I might have stayed out of trouble.

PART III

Back in San Francisco, I considered telling Jenny about Jonathan's papers. It seemed unfair, though, to burden her with my dilemma when she was as distracted as she was. She was spending more time with Tara, making sure to get home earlier from work. Every night, before Tara went to bed, they spent forty-five minutes talking about their day. They'd made it a nightly ritual.

Tara was less sullen than she'd been when she came home from camp, and certainly less so than in New York. She would sit with me in the evening while I read in my bedroom.

"You're losing your hair," she said one night.

"I guess I am."

"Mine's growing back." She tugged on a clump of it, as if she were offering to give me some.

"Are you going to grow it long?"

"Maybe."

I turned to the photograph on the nightstand, of her and Jenny taken the day she was born. "I can see you in that picture," I told her. "You're older and prettier, but you look the same."

She didn't answer, but started reading. I'd lent her my copy of *A Tale of Two Cities*.

After a while I looked over at her. "'It was the best of times, it was the worst of times.' That's one of the most famous opening lines in the English language. Dickens wrote serially. Can you imagine what it's like having to live with your mistakes all the way through a book?"

Tara smiled politely, the way you smile at someone who doesn't know when to stop talking. "I'm going to bed," she told me, and kissed me on the forehead.

At school, I saw my students from the previous year. They'd grown over the summer. A couple of the boys sported mustaches. Several students shook my hand and patted me on the back. Some of the girls kissed me, as though we were old friends.

When school let out for the day, I played pick-up basketball with some of the boys. I was still stronger and quicker than most of them, but when I got the ball they called me Old Man Suskind and said I'd grown up before the jump shot was invented.

For the first week of school I stuck to my routine—teaching, playing basketball, going home to Jenny and Tara. I tried to forget about Jonathan's birth papers but wasn't able to.

I went over to his house one evening in September, having decided to give him the information. Sandy was out, and we made dinner together.

"Cheers," Jonathan said, raising his wineglass in a toast. We were on his deck, overlooking Nineteenth Street. I reached into my pants pocket and gave him the envelope. I was smiling—out of nervousness more than anything else.

"What is this?"

"Just open it."

The papers fell onto his lap. The birth certificate lay on top; the adoption records were folded beneath. "I don't get it."

"It's a birth certificate," I said. "*Your* birth certificate."

"What?"

"Look at it."

He read the name aloud, like someone pulling a piece of paper from a hat and calling out the name of a stranger. "Michael Ivan Harris."

"Look at the birthday."

"December 21, 1964. Oh, God." He was reading but he wasn't, skimming the details, knowing everything at once.

He stood up. I did too. He put his plate on the table. I put mine there as well. I wasn't sure what was about to happen. For all I knew, he was going to hit me. We were reflections of each other, like mimes, standing a few feet apart.

He took a step toward me. I stood still. I saw a bus go by below him. He took another step toward me. He raised his arms. Then he thrust them around me and we were in a hug. His breath came out in tiny shudders. His collarbone was firm against mine. His nose was pressed to my ear. His arms were draped heavily over me.

The hug surprised me—the strength, the duration. His left kneecap was pressed against my right. I smelled soap and after-shave on his neck.

When he stepped back, I saw tears in his eyes. His face looked misshapen.

"I'm sorry, Jon."

"Where did you find this?"

"In storage. In New York."

"Do Mom and Dad know?"

I shook my head.

"Can we keep it a secret?"

I nodded.

He went in and came back with the ice cream I'd brought, which we ate with huge spoons directly from the containers.

"Let's not talk about this," he said. "I want to pretend it didn't happen."

We watched *Monday Night Football* in the bedroom. Jonathan seemed eager to reflect on our childhood, as if to remind himself that it had taken place.

We had the picture on without the volume. The players moved silently across the screen and piled on top of one another.

"Remember Howard Cosell?" he asked. "*Monday Night Football* and the big boxing matches?" He imitated Cosell's voice. "The thrilla in Manilla."

I smiled. "Joe Frazier and Muhammad Ali."

"Ben, did you ever think we'd be where we are now?"

"In San Francisco?"

"You know. Doing what we're doing?"

"I guess not."

"I knew nothing about San Francisco," he said. "I used to call it 'Frisco.' Can you believe it?" He started to sing. "'California, here I come . . .'"

I thought of us in seventh grade, standing together on the stage of the Waldorf-Astoria ballroom, singing songs from *Joseph and the Amazing Technicolor Dreamcoat* at the alumni dinner. We used to wait six hours between eating milk and meat so that the food wouldn't mix in our stomachs. We checked the ingredients on everything we ate. We teamed up to win the National Blessings Bee.

I wanted to tell him that I loved him, that I'd loved him for as long as I could remember. I was a child again. My parents were saying, "Give Jonathan a kiss, tell your brother you love him." I could feel my lips brush against his nose. When had I stopped telling him I loved him? One day had passed, and then the next, and soon it had been years and it was something we didn't do, something it seemed we couldn't do, as if the words themselves refused to be formed, part of an archaic language.

"Tell me," he said, "why do you want me to meet my birth mother? It's almost as if you're egging me on."

"I'm not egging you on. They're your birth papers. It wouldn't have been fair to keep them from you."

"But why are you invested in my doing something? Tell me the real reason. Don't tell me that it's good for me."

He wouldn't have wanted to hear the real reason. My meeting Susan had everything to do with him. Long before she'd come into my life, I'd imagined us finding our roots together. It all came back to him: the fact that this was what we'd shared—being adopted, above everything else—the fact that even now, at thirty-one, I hadn't accepted that we'd grown apart. Despite the evidence—perhaps because of it—I'd refused to change. I didn't dare tell him that I hoped to meet his birth mother too, that I wanted more than anything to know where he was from.

"Do you remember when I came out to you?" he asked. "I was terrified. There were times before that when I wanted to tell you, but I just couldn't."

"I'm sorry," I said. "I didn't mean to make it hard for you."

"It was even worse with Mom and Dad. I'd told you already, and there was no turning back. Sandy was pressuring me to do it. He said that if I didn't come out to Mom and Dad I wasn't serious about him."

Jonathan held his hands out in front of him, the fingers curled up toward the palms. In high school we'd believed that boys looked at their nails by curling their fingers, while girls held their hands out, palms down. That was how you knew that someone was gay, if he looked at his nails the way a girl did. But even then I'd suspected it was a myth. My brother looks at his nails the way I do.

"I like who I am," Jonathan said. "I don't have to explain myself to anyone."

"I like who you are too."

"I can't meet my birth mother, because if I do I'll have to come out to her. I don't want to go through that with a second family."

"I understand."

"I was confused a lot when I was a kid. Overall, though, I have good memories of childhood. A lot of that is thanks to you. But my life didn't stop at seventeen."

"I know." I didn't think I was telling him that it did, though I understood why he thought I was.

"The present is crazy enough," he said, "without having to worry about the past. I'm around death all the time. In this neighborhood. At the office—"

"I know. I've always admired the work you do. I haven't known how to tell you that without sounding corny or patronizing."

He got up and walked around the bedroom. Then he sat back down. "I remember our time together as kids. I think about you more than you realize." He spoke with a calmness unfamiliar to me. There was an intimacy between us I didn't remember since childhood. I wanted more than anything to reach out and touch him, but I was paralyzed, afraid.

"But then I'm thrown back to the present," he said. "Maybe it's survivors' guilt. Everyone around you is dying, and you wonder why you've been spared."

"What survivors' guilt?"

"That I'm HIV-negative. That Sandy is too."

My body deflated, as if I'd been holding my breath for eleven years, ever since the night he'd come out to me. I stumbled as I stood up. I threw my arms around him. "You're not going to die."

"Not anytime soon."

"I've been afraid about this since college."

"You shouldn't have been. You know me. I've always been cautious."

"You weren't afraid?"

"Not for ages."

I realized what he was telling me. He hadn't just been tested—he'd known for a while.

"When did you find out?"

"I can't even remember. 1987? 1988? After Sandy and I got back together."

I couldn't believe it. I'd been afraid for no reason. Why, I asked him, hadn't he told me, when he'd known how worried I'd been? Didn't he remember that brunch at college when I'd tried to talk to him about AIDS? Did he realize how worried our parents had been—our mother, who left a condom on his nightstand, who, I told him now, had written me at Yale asking me to talk to him about this?

Jonathan looked guarded again, defensive. "It's my private life," he said. "It was up to me whether to tell people."

"But we're your family. Who do you think would have taken care of you if you'd gotten sick?"

"Sandy."

"And if Sandy had gotten sick? When you had that fever last month, I thought you were dying."

"Dying? I had the flu."

"I thought it was the beginning of something worse."

He laughed. "Whenever a gay man gets sick, everyone's imagination takes over. Gay people get colds too, you know."

"Sometimes they get something much worse than that."

"Well, I'm fine. I'm as healthy as you are. In any case, this is what I've been trying to tell you. Sandy and I have had good luck. If we were a few years older—sexually active before people figured out what was going on—there's a good chance we'd both be dead. Or if we hadn't met each other and settled down, we might have ended up sleeping with a lot more men, and who knows what would have happened? People think AIDS is about promiscuity, but it's just as much about luck. There are guys out there who've had unprotected sex hundreds of times with HIV-positive men and have stayed negative. And there are guys who've made just one mistake, and boom, that's it. Life's unfair. I truly believe that. That's why I don't understand your return to God—even if it's not a real return. And that's why I'm not interested in meeting my birth mother. I don't care how things might have been. Already, without meeting her, I can think of so many ways things might have been, it's enough to make a person dizzy. So what I'm saying is, That's that. Case closed. All right?"

"All right," I said, believing it was.

I telephoned my mother at work the next morning to tell her what I'd found out. I was still relieved, still angry.

She was quiet on the other end. Then she started to cry. "God, Ben, I've been so scared."

"Me too."

"I started to say something to him many times, but I could never do it." She took a quick breath. "What about Sandy?"

"He's negative too."

"Thank God."

Then she asked me when Jonathan had found out.

"Last month." I didn't have the heart to tell her the truth.

"Have you told Dad?"

"You tell him." I couldn't imagine talking about this with him, talking with him about anything that had to do with sex.

My mother repeated an ancient Greek saying that my father had once told us: In times of peace sons bury their parents, but in times of war parents bury their sons. "I've thought a lot about that," she said. "I've told myself that all over the world parents bury their kids. As if that would have made it any easier if something had happened to Jonathan."

It was almost eight o'clock. I would be late for work. I told my mother I had to go.

"Talk to me a minute longer," she said. "I need to hear your voice."

Because of vacation and members' kids going back to school, my adoptees' support group had been on hiatus. But in October, we started to meet again. I told everyone that I'd found Jonathan's papers, and this divided the group into two camps. Most members argued that Jonathan was entitled not to meet his birth mother. But a few people said he was denying his true self and it was my job to enlighten him.

"We should never support ignorance." This was Phillip, a man about my age, who had met his birth mother when he was twenty, his birth father when he was twenty-five. "In any case, it's not just a question of what's best for your brother, but of what's best for you. It's a question of what's best for all of us."

"For all of us?" I said.

"What your brother does has ramifications." Phillip saw our support group as part of a movement. The greater the number of adoptees who found their birth parents, the more attention adoption would receive and the easier it would be to get birth records opened. In the process, society would be sensitized to the needs of adoptees and to the fact that there were many different kinds of families. We were like any other movement, he told the group. In a way we resembled the gay rights movement. He even used the word "closeted" to refer to Jonathan and suggested that he needed to be outed.

"My brother isn't closeted," I said. "He's never denied that he's adopted."

"He may not deny it in the narrow sense, but he denies it more fundamentally."

Phillip appealed to my vanity, telling me that I had done the noble thing while Jonathan had taken the easy way out. And when I told the group that I was interested in meeting Jonathan's birth mother, I found an ally in Phillip.

"You can search for her yourself," he said.

"Me?"

"Why not? If you think you should know, and I can see a good argument for that—he's your brother, after all—then you should do it."

I kept thinking about this the next few weeks. Why shouldn't I search for her? Jonathan didn't have to find out. God knew he wasn't hesitant to keep secrets from me. We were both adults. We'd each do as we wanted.

I had off from school on election day, and I took Susan with me when I went to vote.

"Are you registered in San Francisco?" I asked. If she was, I thought, it would be a clear sign that she was staying indefinitely.

"No."

"Did you vote absentee?"

"I should have. My husband has been giving me a hard time about it."

So she was still in touch with him.

At her apartment, she made me lunch.

"I found Jonathan's birth records," I said. I considered telling her I might search for his birth mother, but she would have been offended. I hadn't even searched for her.

"Where did you find them?"

"In New York." I had an image of myself sitting in front of the storage closet, discovering that Jonathan had been called Michael. I asked Susan if she'd given me another name. It had never occurred to me before.

"Your name was Christopher."

I let the word slide across my lips. "Christopher." A Christian name.

"But I didn't call you anything for the first couple of weeks because I didn't want to get too attached to you."

"And after that?"

"It seemed silly. I was attached to you already and you were still there. I hadn't found the right parents for you."

I hadn't realized that she'd considered other couples. I'd simply imagined an adoption line with my parents at the front of it.

"Then I met your parents, and I liked them. They were responsible and financially secure. They seemed concerned about me."

"You met them?" They'd made my birth mother out to be almost mythic, a mere metaphor for my dark past. I'd practically come to believe that I'd grown on a tree and that my parents had plucked me from it.

"They came to New Jersey," Susan said, "and we spent the afternoon together."

"Did they meet my birth father?"

She shook her head. "He was gone. He turned eighteen and was off to the Marines."

Susan excused herself and left the kitchen, then came back a minute later with an envelope. "Open it," she said.

Inside was an old photo, the colors bleeding across the paper. A girl was holding a baby. My mother and father stood on either side of her.

"It's you and me," Susan said, "with your parents."

Everyone looked so young. My parents were smiling, but Susan's face was drawn. She must have been thinking that this was the last time she'd hold me. It was strange to see them together, the different reactions to the same event, as though two photographs had been blended. I was two months old, and asleep. It might have been the oldest picture of me that existed.

I tried to recall my first impression of Susan that day she'd walked into the Ethiopian restaurant. "You thought about keeping me, didn't you?" I asked.

"Of course I did."

"But?"

"I didn't really have a choice. My parents wouldn't let me."

"And if they had?"

"I probably still would have given you up. It was the right thing to do. For both of us. But I wish my parents hadn't forced me. That way I wouldn't have spent so much time persuading myself that I'd have made a different decision." The lines near her mouth looked etched in; she seemed to have aged in the last several months.

"What about abortion?"

"I couldn't do it."

"Why not?"

"Because for a long time I pretended I wasn't pregnant, and by the time I admitted it, it was too late. Besides, I'm Catholic."

"You're opposed to abortion?"

"Except for rape and incest."

"Well, I'm happy I wasn't the product of rape or incest." I was trying to lighten the mood. But the words came out clunky and badly timed.

"Did you use contraception?" Some Catholics wouldn't, I knew.

Susan looked embarrassed. Could I blame her? I was asking her for answers I only half wanted, talking about things we shouldn't have been discussing.

But she answered me. Perhaps she felt she had to. "We used rubbers."

A shudder of discomfort ran through me. Maybe this was a sign that she really was my mother: I was embarrassed to think of her having sex.

"I don't want to discuss this," Susan said.

She was right.

She told me she knew I'd written her husband. She spoke without a hint of emotion. She was making me wait. And I was behaving like the person I was—a squirming son, caught by his mother. "How did you get his address?"

"I assumed it was the same as yours," I answered.

"Why did you write him?"

I could have told her I hadn't been thinking. But I had to do better than that. "I know this doesn't make sense to you, but I feel partly responsible for the problems in your marriage. You left your husband and came to see me."

"That doesn't mean you caused our problems."

"I was just trying to help." Although this sounded absurd, it was true.

"If anything, it made matters worse."

"Come on," I said.

"Why did you think it would help? You're a stranger to Frank, and he doesn't like strangers knowing about his marital problems. I had to assure him that I hadn't set this up."

"Set it up?"

"He thought I asked you to write the letter—that it was my way of telling him I was still thinking about him. Frank thought you were being patronizing."

"I know. He wrote me."

"He did?"

I nodded.

"Look how out of hand this is getting. You've gotten us into an absurd triangle."

"I'm sorry. I shouldn't have written him. But I don't know why he thought I was being patronizing."

"He didn't like your comment about *The American Spectator*."

"What comment?"

She walked out of the kitchen and returned holding my letter. Frank must have mailed it to her. "'I was at her apartment recently, and she was reading a copy of *The American Spectator*. She appreciates the subscription you gave her. She enjoys the magazine.'"

I told her she was right. It was a silly comment.

"It was also a lie. I don't enjoy the magazine, and you know it. Frank thought your comment was snide. He realizes your politics are different from his."

"He has no way of knowing that."

"Come on, Ben. You're a Jewish kid from Manhattan."

I was tempted to tell her she was being anti-Semitic, but it was neither true nor to the point.

"The fact is, you *can* be patronizing. Like those comments about my earrings."

"What comments? I've been supportive of your work. I've told you that. I feel bad that you got pregnant and your career was derailed."

"You imagine my career was derailed. I never said anything about it. You like that I might have been a famous artist. As if having a birth mother who's just a normal person wouldn't be good enough for you."

"Look, Susan, I'm sorry I wrote your husband. I don't know what else to tell you."

I continued to think about Jonathan's birth papers, so I called information in Chicago and asked for a listing for Alfred and Rebecca Harris. This was just exploratory. I was simply finding out what was possible.

No Alfred Harris was listed. Two Rebecca Harrises were, one of them with an unpublished number. The operator gave me the published number and address.

I considered throwing the information out, but changed my mind. Had Jonathan been interested in my past, he'd have done what I was doing—and without telling me. The man with a million secrets. And what were the chances of my finding his birth mother? He'd been born more than thirty years ago.

I could write this woman and tell her the truth—that she might have given birth to my brother and that I hoped to meet her. But that wouldn't work. She may not have wanted to meet Jonathan; she surely didn't want to meet me, someone who would remind her of what had happened without allowing her to see the child she'd given up.

So I wrote this letter.

Dear Mr. and Mrs. Harris,

Almost thirty-one years ago in Chicago, I was born to you, I believe. I have often wondered who and where you are. I live in San Francisco, but I'd be willing to fly to Chicago to meet you. Don't worry, I won't disrupt your life. I'm not looking for money or any other kind of help. I just want to ask you some questions. If you don't want to meet me I'll understand, but I hope you'll agree to my request. I look forward to hearing from you.

Yours truly,
Jonathan Suskind

I addressed an envelope and put my work address in the upper left-hand corner. I didn't want a response to come to the apartment.

I started checking the mail two days later. Everything, I imagined, was being sped up for me. The postal service had suspended other operations and was concentrating solely on my correspondence.

Already, after a week, I started to feel foolish. Of course I had the wrong Rebecca Harris.

In the days that followed, I again thought of confiding in Jenny. But every time I was about to, I changed my mind. The day she came home having lost her rape case, I knew I'd made the right decision. She was upset at herself for having let her client down. She was distracted and testy.

"It's not just that I lost. It's that I went through the motions."

"At least it's over."

"What about the next one? The cases are only going to get tougher."

"The guy was guilty, Jen. No one could have gotten him off."

"That's no excuse for not doing my best."

"Besides, he's violent and dangerous. You don't want him on the streets."

"I can't think that way. If I start thinking about who I want on the streets, I won't be able to defend anyone."

I tried to comfort her, but I couldn't.

After work the next day, I went to the library and looked up Jenny's name on Lexis and Nexis. She'd been quoted in the newspapers several times in articles about cases she was working on, and received compliments from her clients and other lawyers. "Principled." "A brilliant young defense attorney." There had been a feature on her in the *San Jose Mercury News*, under the title "Head of Her Class." I made copies of these articles and highlighted what had been said about her, then brought them home and spread them across her desk.

During Christmas season, Jenny and I got into an argument again. She and Tara were driving to Half Moon Bay to get a tree for our apartment. They invited me along, but I didn't want to go.

This was my first Christmas living with them. I'd known they celebrated Christmas; every year, the week after Thanksgiving, they drove to Half Moon Bay to cut their own tree. Why, then, was I surprised? Did I expect this year to be different?

But it *was* different. I lived with them. I had nothing against Christmas, as long as I wasn't involved with it. Now the tree would be in my home.

Jenny had agreed to have a mezuzah on our doorpost and occasionally to celebrate the sabbath. The least I could do was not object to a Christmas tree.

But I thought of Christmas trees as bottom-line. I was a history teacher. Judaism was about nothing if not history. That history included centuries of anti-Semitism. The Crusades. The Spanish Inquisition. The Holocaust. These lessons had been hammered into me all my life. To a Jew like me, Christmas was a reminder that I was a stranger in a strange land. It was about being swallowed up.

Jenny couldn't understand this.

"This isn't about God," she told me. She and Tara had come

home with the tree, which they'd tied like a deer to the roof of Jenny's car. "Besides, Christmas trees are pagan symbols. They have nothing to do with Christianity."

"The Jews had trouble with the pagans too."

"The Jews had trouble with everybody. If you gave everyone a hard time who's descended from an anti-Semite, you wouldn't have any friends left."

"I'm not trying to give you a hard time."

"Well, you are." She'd placed the tree upright and was wiping the sap off her clothes.

"This isn't about you, Jen, and it isn't about individual Christians. It isn't even about Christianity itself, which is practiced by many people I respect."

"Well, then?"

"It's about my being involved in this. It's not my holiday, and I don't want to pretend it is."

"I'm not asking you to pretend it's your holiday. I'm just asking you to recognize that it's my holiday."

"I do."

"And even if I didn't care about having a tree, Tara does. I won't deprive her of it. Considering all we've done when it comes to Judaism, you're being a little stingy."

"I know. I'm sorry."

But I couldn't get beyond it.

For the next few weeks, I said nothing more about the tree. Still I resented it, and Jenny noticed. Our conversations were barbed; we snapped at each other.

One night, I moved the tree to another corner of the room. It was casting shadows across the TV set while I was trying to watch the Golden State Warriors on TNT.

Jenny came in and glared at me. "How much basketball can a person watch?"

"If you knew how little basketball I watched compared to a lot of other people . . ."

"I don't live with other people. I live with you."

"Well, no one's asking you to watch it."

On Christmas Eve, I sat in the living room and didn't say anything while Jenny and Tara decorated the tree.

"Stop moping," Jenny said.

"I'm not moping."

"You certainly are."

"What would you like me to do? Get up and dance? Sing 'The Twelve Days of Christmas'?"

"I don't care what you do. But if you're going to be the grinch, just leave."

"Right now?"

"Why not? Go off for the evening, and come back when this is over. Everyone will be happier."

I left abruptly and slammed the door behind me. I walked to Jonathan and Sandy's. I'd betrayed Jonathan by writing to Rebecca Harris, and there I was, turning to him for comfort.

I told him about my argument with Jenny.

"It's just a tree," he said.

"Come on. It's a lot more than that. What if Sandy wanted a tree?"

"But I don't," Sandy said.

"What if you did?" I turned to Jonathan. "Would that be okay with you?"

"Why not? I can tell you one thing. I wouldn't make a huge fuss about it."

Hearing this saddened me, as if years before we hadn't spent Christmas Day in a movie theater, watching a series of double features in order to drown out the holiday. Senior year of high school, on Christmas, we'd taken the bus to Atlantic City and sneaked into Bally's. Christmas: the one day when, according to tradition, Jews were allowed to gamble. In the darkened mirrored hallways of the casino there were so many yarmulkes by the slot machines you might have thought that this was our holiday, that we were there for a Jewish convention.

"Well, don't invite *me* to your Christmas party," I said.

"Come on," said Sandy. "Lighten up."

I left their house a little before midnight and thought of going home. But I didn't want to fight with Jenny. It was better to wait until she'd gone to sleep. Overhead, clouds had settled along Twin Peaks, and as I walked down the hill it started to rain. The slick marks of tires shone beneath the traffic lights. Most of the stores on Market Street were closed. There was no line at the Wells Fargo cash machine. On the corner of Market and Castro, a couple of teenagers were listening to music on a boom box. Aside from them, the neighborhood was quiet.

I decided to go see Susan. Maybe being with her on Christmas Eve would give me a better sense of the meaning of Christmas, especially since she was religious. That was part of my problem—I was Orthodox at heart. The synagogue I didn't go to was Orthodox. Despite my own practices, I had an all-or-nothing attitude. Either you were religious or you weren't. The true Christians, the ones who went to church and believed in God, who were active all year and not just on Christmas, they alone were allowed a Christmas tree. For them Christmas wasn't a fake holiday. It wasn't just the windows of Lord & Taylor and the Rudolph the Red-Nosed Reindeer TV specials.

I walked to Twenty-fourth Street, then turned east. On Valencia, I stopped at a phone booth to call Susan. I let the phone ring several times; she didn't answer. Maybe she was asleep, or at midnight mass. Maybe she was at home but just wasn't picking up.

When I got to her apartment I rang the buzzer. She didn't come down and let me in. I rang several more times, then sat on her stoop, waiting for her to return.

The rain had started to fall again, making patterns near my feet and seeping through my sneakers. It was almost one in the morning. I wished I could be many things at once: Susan's child and my parents' child, someone who went to synagogue but didn't mind a Christmas tree in his home.

A man walked past me holding a bottle of beer. He moved slowly, swaying from side to side. A car drove by. The streetlights were dull, the buildings along Susan's block formless.

I sat there until one-thirty, when Susan got home, dropped off by a cab. She was wearing a gray wool skirt and a dark blazer. She was searching for the keys in her pocketbook and didn't notice me sitting on the stoop.

"Hi, Susan. Are you coming from church?"

"God, Ben. You scared me. Yes, I'm coming from church." She looked at her watch. "It's one-thirty in the morning. Is everything all right?"

"Everything's fine."

"Then why aren't you home? Where are Jenny and Tara?"

"I wanted to see you."

"At one-thirty in the morning?"

"Do you want me to leave?"

"No, it's fine. You just surprised me, that's all."

She invited me inside. A small, undecorated Christmas tree stood next to the window in a corner of her living room. The apartment looked sparser than when I'd last seen it. It had a somber air, perhaps because Christmas was supposed to be a family holiday. It was sad to celebrate it alone. On the table in front of the wicker rocking chair sat a solitary copy of the Bible. It reminded me of a motel room.

"Were you planning to do Bible study?" I asked. I had no idea what people did on Christmas Eve.

Susan smiled. "It's almost two in the morning, Ben. I was planning to go to sleep."

"I'm sorry. I'll leave." I got up to go.

"No." She raised her hand to stop me. "That wasn't what I meant. I was just saying you haven't interrupted anything."

I sat down again.

"I got into a fight with Jenny," I said.

"About what?"

"Christmas. Christmas trees, actually—specifically the one in our apartment. But there's always more to these fights. It's really about my willingness to compromise. Jenny thinks that I'm being a prick, and in this case, it's hard to deny it."

"You're not a prick."

"Thank you. But I can see how Jenny would think I am. It comes down to reason—and I think I'm generally a reasonable person—versus principle. What it really comes down to is whether Jenny and I are compatible."

"You don't want a Christmas tree in your apartment?"

"No."

I explained to her that by coming to see her I was hoping to get a better sense of what Christmas was like. "I know. It's ridiculous. If I truly wanted to get a better sense of Christmas, I should have gone with you to church. What did I expect to find here? Christmas is supposed to be a family holiday, and your family is in Indiana. You probably aren't happy spending it alone."

"You're part of my family."

I didn't respond.

I flipped through her Bible as if to glean some lesson from it. I lay down on the sofa and closed my eyes. "I'd like you to tell me some Christmas stories. Not traditional ones—baby in the manger and stuff like that. Just stories about Christmas when you were growing up. Better yet, tell me what Christmas is like with your family."

I realized this was a lot to ask. Two Christmases before, Scottie had been alive. The memories must have been painful.

I no longer remember what she told me that night, because even at the time I was focused more on the sound of her voice than on what she was actually telling me. *Hush. Moonlight. Candied ham. Waking up early Christmas morning. The creaking of narrow stairs.* I lay on the sofa until three in the morning, listening to her talk.

It was almost four when I got home. I was feeling conciliatory, less because of anything that had happened at Susan's than because of fatigue and the passage of time, because of the sense that I'd blown things out of proportion—that Jenny and I would work something out.

But Jenny was still awake and not feeling conciliatory. "Look at you. I've never seen anything more pathetic in my life. Have you been wandering around in the rain, looking for other people who hate Christmas?"

"No," I said, "I haven't."

"You've been gone for hours. I thought maybe you'd flown off to Israel so you could be with a whole country of people who hate Christmas."

"That's very smart, Jen. As you might recall, Jerusalem's a holy place for Christians too. And Bethlehem is just a stone's throw away."

"All right. Drop it."

"Look, I'm sorry for how I handled this. If I could do it over, I would."

I told her that next year we would work out a compromise. We could have the tree in the apartment, only maybe she'd consider keeping it for less time—just the week of Christmas perhaps. I, in turn, would be respectful of her holiday. I'd even try to join in.

"I don't know if there will be a next year."

"What's that supposed to mean?"

"I'm not sure we're going to be together."

"Because of this?"

"Because of the bigger problems beneath it."

This scared me. We'd always known that things might not work out, but this was the first time she'd said she was thinking of leaving me. Suddenly the tree seemed insignificant. I didn't want to lose her over something like this. I didn't want to lose her, period.

When I got back to work after New Year's, I found an envelope in my box with handwriting startlingly similar to my brother's. Inside was a letter.

Dear Mr. Suskind,

I received your note last month, and I've been thinking about it ever since. I never expected to hear from you. Yes, I gave birth to you, but if you knew the circumstances, you'd understand why I gave you up—it was the only real option for everyone involved. I thought I found good parents for you. I certainly did my best. I've spent many years trying to forget about you, but I haven't slept much since I got your letter, so maybe you're right—maybe it's best for me to know who you are.

I'm willing to meet you. But only on the condition that you keep this a secret. No one else knows you exist. I eat lunch every weekday between one and two at a restaurant in Chicago named Pauline's. You can find it in information. There's no need to write me back. I'm not going anywhere. You can just show up, and I'll be there.

Cordially,
Rebecca Harris

She hadn't mentioned Alfred or the fact that my letter had been addressed to them both. She'd left it up to me—I didn't *have* to go to Chicago. All I'd done was send her a letter to which I hadn't expected a response.

But it wasn't fair to tease her like that. That was what I told myself—to justify my plans. Also, what if months passed without my showing up? She might write me again to see what had happened. She might look Jonathan up in San Francisco information and call him. I was locked in now. I had to follow through.

Her letter intrigued me. " . . . if you knew the circumstances, you'd understand why I gave you up." What circumstances? And why did this have to be a secret? She ate every day at the same restaurant. She sounded like she was in the Mafia.

I made a plane reservation for two weeks later. I'd fly to Chicago on Sunday and spend the night in a hotel. Monday was Martin Luther King Day, and school would be closed. I'd take Tuesday as a sick day and fly back to California that night.

I wrote her a short note.

Dear Mrs. Harris,

I received your letter, and I'm glad you have agreed to meet me. I expect to come to Chicago soon.

Best wishes,
Jonathan Suskind

I was fidgety and nervous till I left. I spent my evenings pacing around the living room, opening and closing closet doors, flipping through channels on TV.

"What's wrong?" Jenny asked.

"Nothing. I'm fine."

The week before I left, I told Jenny I had to fly to Chicago.

"For what?"

"A teachers' meeting."

"In Chicago?"

"It's a national teachers' meeting."

She wondered why I hadn't mentioned it before.

"I didn't know about it," I said. "Someone else was supposed to go, but she got sick. They asked me to replace her."

"Did you have to say yes?"

I nodded.

She looked at me dubiously.

"Believe me, Jen, I wish I didn't have to." My voice sickened me. Yet I carried on.

On the plane to Chicago, I ate my kosher meal and tried to fall asleep. I was scared by what I was doing, unsure about how I'd gotten from there to here. This was how such decisions were made. Only in retrospect did you realize you'd made them. When we were little, the walk to synagogue was long for Jonathan and me, so my father used to tell us to think of it as a block at a time; no single block was too long or difficult. The same was true here. Piece by piece. Divide and conquer. Until the decision was so fragmented it didn't feel like one. You met your birth mother. You encouraged your brother to meet his. You found his birth certificate and gave it to him. You considered finding his birth parents. You called an operator and took down an address. You wrote a letter. You got one back. Each of the steps seemed insignificant until they'd been added up and you realized you'd been moving inexorably forward.

So there I was, still with the chance to turn back, but also with the compulsion to continue. By finding out who Jonathan had been I might learn something about who he was now. And then, maybe, I could put things to rest.

But I was terrified. What if my plane crashed? The truth would come out—there had been no teachers' meeting—and Jenny would spend the rest of her life not knowing why I'd gone to Chicago. Had I been having an affair? I'd be dead, of course, unable to worry, but I was alive now, plenty capable of worrying about my dead self and how he would be remembered by the world.

Mrs. Harris might not believe I was Jonathan. His eyes were lighter than mine, and he had a mole on the side of his neck.

"What happened to your eyes?" she would ask me.

"They got darker," I would say. "A baby's eyes almost always do."

"What happened to your mole?"

"I had it removed."

We'd be sitting at Pauline's. Everyone who ate there would be sitting alone; it would be a haunt for spies and organized criminals. They would wear sunglasses and smoke cigars; above the bar would be a set of antlers. The windows would be tinted like those of limousines, and the waiters, out of fear and respect, would look down at their polished black shoes when they took your order.

I arrived at O'Hare, rented a car, and checked into a hotel. I turned on the TV and fell asleep on one bed with my clothes still on and the contents of my bag strewn across the other bed.

The next morning I drove into the city. On the radio, the mayor of Chicago was talking about the legacy of Martin Luther King, Jr., and the work that was still to be done. Teenagers were playing basketball, skidding on the ice as they shot lay-ups.

I drove out to the suburbs, to Oak Park, past Ernest Hemingway's birthplace and the Frank Lloyd Wright houses. I circled back to the city and parked near the Art Institute. It had been months since I'd been to a museum, and I had no special interest in this one. I seemed determined to be a tourist, to pretend I was there for reasons other than the real one. I went into the museum, walked around for ten minutes, and left.

At one o'clock, I stood in front of Pauline's, checking my reflection in the window. Maybe Mrs. Harris wouldn't be there; perhaps she didn't work on Martin Luther King Day.

Pauline's wasn't a haunt for organized criminals. It didn't have tinted windows, or antlers on the walls. It was so ordinary it might have been part of a chain of luncheonettes—something you saw in the basement of a shopping mall, Indian food next to Chinese next to bagels next to pizza next to frozen yogurt.

The floors were white tile and the bare walls looked scrubbed. The place smelled antiseptic and was illuminated by parallel sets of long fluorescent light bulbs. The food was served cafeteria style. I couldn't imagine anyone eating there every day, much less Jonathan's birth mother—Jonathan, who in college had brewed his own beer, who for his thirtieth birthday had gotten a set of Thai cookbooks and Thai cooking lessons from Sandy.

The restaurant was long and narrow. It turned at a right angle past the food counter, then at a right angle again. It was like an obstacle course, the chairs and tables arranged indiscriminately.

I saw myself doing what I'd done years before. "Excuse me," I'd say, moving from customer to customer, "are you my mother?"

Although no one in the restaurant looked like Jonathan, there were several women about the right age. I stopped in front of one of them. "Excuse me," I said, "are you Rebecca Harris?"

"No," the woman said, sounding slightly annoyed, as if she were always being mistaken for Rebecca Harris—as if this were an occupational hazard of eating at Pauline's.

"I'm Rebecca Harris," a woman called out. She was at another table, several yards away, and appeared no more surprised than the first woman had been, as though she too were used to having strangers ask whether she was Rebecca Harris. She stared at me without a touch of inquisitiveness—without any emotion, it seemed—like a statue of who she was, a woman in a bad restaurant holding her soup spoon in midair.

The first thing I thought was, This is a mistake. She looked nothing like Jonathan. I was convinced she was playing a prank on me, retaliating for my deception.

"Mrs. Harris," I said, "I'm Jonathan Suskind." I was astonished by how easily these words came out, by how quickly and unashamedly

I took to the role. Rebecca Harris was small, heavyset, and not especially attractive. Her hair was mostly gray and she wore bifocals. She reminded me of a school nurse. Her skin was pale and her eyes were grayish-green. There was something indeterminate about the way she looked, like those 3-D baseball cards I used to find in cereal boxes, with faces that changed when you held them at different angles. She must have been at least sixty years old. No one would have mistaken her for my sister; no one could have thought we were on a date.

She put down her soup spoon. "Goodness." A bead of sweat trickled down her forehead. Her hair looked like it had been set with bobby pins.

I reached out to shake her hand. She squeezed it firmly. I took a step closer to her, as if I really thought she was a nurse and was expecting her to examine me.

She seemed as surprised by me as I was by her. I worried that I'd betrayed my identity, like someone who's just come from a conference and forgotten to remove his name tag.

"Mr. Suskind," she said.

"Jonathan."

"Jonathan," she repeated.

I was excited by the lie I was telling. My identity really was fungible. I could say anything here, and no one would know. Looking at the mirror behind her, I almost expected to see myself transmogrified, actually melting into Jonathan.

"You said I could come here." I sounded more defensive than I'd intended to. I pointed to the floor where I was standing, as if she didn't realize where I was.

Mrs. Harris stood up, indicated the seat opposite hers, and sat down again. She pushed her tray aside, and picked up a folder that had been lying on the floor and placed it on the table between us. She smiled politely at me the way an interviewer would. Was she going to produce my résumé?

"Weren't you expecting me?"

"Of course I was." Her voice was even, unmodulated.

"But not yet?"

"I expected you to come sometime." Her face softened briefly. But then it turned tight. She sat up straight, like a mannequin.

A man walked by, his tray casting diagonal shadows along the table and reflecting in the mirrors. Mrs. Harris rested her hands flat on the table, which was made of the kind of wood usually used for picnic benches. It was distinctly out of place. People had carved figures into the top, and between Mrs. Harris's hands was a big heart with the words "Diane & Hud" inside it.

"Well, here I am." I'd been waiting for this moment, but now that I was here it felt anticlimactic. Maybe it would have been better to have gotten someone else to point Mrs. Harris out to me. I could have examined her from afar and left. I had all these questions to ask her, but it was as if I were standing at the front of a lecture hall and being required to speak in Japanese.

Mrs. Harris's hands still rested next to her soup bowl. I didn't understand how she could seem so calm. I felt offended for Jonathan, and by association for me.

When Susan had met me, she'd told me to call her by her first name. But Mrs. Harris hadn't asked me to call her Rebecca. She sat before me, hazy and stout, making me wonder what the years had done to her. I had the inexplicable urge to call her Mom.

I stood up. I wasn't hungry, but I couldn't just sit there doing nothing with my hands. Maybe Mrs. Harris would resume eating if I too had some food before me.

I came back with a roast beef sandwich and a can of Dr Pepper. "This is a nice place," I said. On the table next to ours was an abandoned tray that held a plate of congealing meat loaf and a few overcooked pieces of carrot.

"Where's my birth father?" I asked. I thought of my own birth father shooting baskets on the courts outside his high school.

"Mr. Harris?"

"I wrote both of you."

"My husband's dead."

"Oh God. I'm sorry."

"It happened a long time ago. The summer of 1974."

I was only ten, I thought.

"It was the day Nixon resigned," she said. "My husband was just sitting in the living room, and he dropped dead of a heart attack."

"I'm really sorry." The day Nixon resigned, Jonathan and I had watched my parents rejoice. My mother did a jig when she heard the news. Now I wondered what my brother had been thinking. Was it possible that he'd sensed something was wrong?

"He was forty-one years old," Mrs. Harris said. "The same thing happened to his brother."

"A heart attack?"

She nodded.

I worried for Jonathan. Arteriosclerosis. Clogged arteries. High cholesterol. I didn't know what his cholesterol was. We played basketball together; he was lean and in good shape. But he ate a lot of meat and cheese. I'd brought ice cream to dinner that night. I was helping to kill him.

Mrs. Harris took out her wallet. "That's your birth father." She pointed at a photograph. "Twenty-two years later I still carry him with me."

I was so startled I gasped.

"What's wrong?"

The picture looked so much like Jonathan it could have been of him. "He was a very handsome man."

"Thank you." Hearing me say this seemed to make her relax. She put her folder back on the floor. I wanted to ask what was inside it. Why she had placed it on the table like something she wanted to refer to?

"Mrs. Harris," I said, "will you tell me what happened?" We'd been at Pauline's for half an hour, and suddenly she was more attractive to me. Her face had opened up. People never look the way they do when you first meet them. No one stays the same.

"It's only fair," she said. "You flew across the country. But you have to promise me something. You can't track any more of us down."

"Any more of you?"

"Promise me."

I had no idea what she meant, but I promised.

She looked around to make sure no one was listening, then leaned forward and lowered her voice. "I gave birth to you on December 21, 1964."

"Right."

"But everything happened in secret."

"Why?"

She moved her hand back and forth across the table, like someone dusting crumbs into a pile. I realized how hard this was for her, how she was doing her best not to cry.

"Your birth father was an engineer," Mrs. Harris said, "but he got laid off from his job and couldn't find another one. Times were bad. We had loans to pay and two kids to support. We were in serious trouble."

"Two kids?"

"A boy and a girl."

"I had a brother and a sister?"

"You still do."

I couldn't believe it. Jonathan had two siblings he didn't know about. In a way I did too. I imagined the four of us living together, renting a house in Chicago. Perhaps Jonathan would feel a kinship with them, something deeper than he and I had.

"Where are they now?"

"I can't tell you that." Her voice was firm. "They don't know you exist. No one does."

She was six months pregnant, she told me, when her husband lost his job. It was too late to get an abortion. The family was in debt and had to sell the furniture. Collectors were knocking on the front door. Their only choice was to give me up. Her husband was embarrassed that he couldn't support the family, so he persuaded her to tell people she had miscarried.

"You lied?" I didn't have a right to feel shocked by this. Everything I'd done since I'd written her had been a colossal lie.

"It was awful. I had to go through a fake mourning, all the while knowing the real mourning lay ahead, when I'd have you in secret and give you up."

I felt a flash of anger, as if she really had killed Jonathan off. She stared back at me—amazed, it seemed, that I existed. Had she come to believe her own story?

"Didn't people suspect?"

"Some did. I'm sure the neighbors wondered. But I stayed home all the time and the kids were still small. They were too young to understand what was happening."

"They still don't know?"

Mrs. Harris shook her head. "You lie to someone long enough and it gets harder to change your story."

I thought of my parents' lie—how as time passed they probably started to forget, how it became easier to believe that I'd been born Jewish.

"Besides, I never thought I'd see you."

She was right—she wouldn't have. If I hadn't flown here and pretended I was Jonathan, she wouldn't be thinking about any of this. I felt terrible. I'd been so focused on lying to Jenny, so focused on deceiving Jonathan, that I hadn't considered Mrs. Harris. She'd been an abstraction before I met her.

"Three months after we gave you up," she said, "your birth father got another job. Things worked out for us. I kept thinking that maybe we could get you back. But I knew it wouldn't work. And besides, it didn't seem fair to your new parents. Then Alfred died nine years later, and I knew we'd made the right decision. It was hard enough on your brother and sister. Why put another child through that?"

"You did the right thing," I said.

"I did? I thought you came here because you were upset. You read about kids finding their birth parents and blaming them for giving them up."

"I don't blame you. I love my parents. They've been good to me."

Mrs. Harris seemed relieved.

"Tell me something," I said. "Are you Jewish?" This was the question I'd most wanted to ask. But I didn't know what answer to wish for. Instinctively I hoped that she'd say she was Jewish—that not everything my parents had told us had been a lie.

"I don't practice any religion."

"But were you born Jewish?"

She nodded.

"And my birth father?"

"He was Jewish too."

Jonathan was a Jew. Why, then, did I feel disappointed? It may have been envy, or simply anticlimax. But it's occurred to me since then that, until that moment, I'd allowed myself to believe that we really were related.

"Tell me about you," Mrs. Harris said. "How long have you lived in San Francisco? Do you have a career?"

I tried to answer as Jonathan would. I wanted to protect myself and be honest with Mrs. Harris. I wanted to leave her with at least a shard of the truth.

"I'm a doctor," I said.

"What kind?"

"A geriatrician. I've been in San Francisco since I graduated from college."

"Do you have a family?"

"A what?"

"You know. A wife and children."

I hesitated. If Jonathan had known what I was doing, would he have wanted me to come out to her? Did I owe it to him to tell her the truth? Did I owe it to Mrs. Harris?

"I'm not married," I said.

"Do you have a girlfriend?"

"No."

"There's still time," she said, as if to comfort me.

I smiled at her and told her she was right.

I was spent. So was Mrs. Harris. Her gray hair was damp and matted to her forehead. Smoking wasn't allowed in the restaurant, but a woman at the next table lit up a cigarette. She waved the smoke dismissively from in front of her face, as if she didn't know how it had gotten there. A janitor was mopping the floor. This appeared to be a hint that it was closing time, but it was only two o'clock.

"You had an older brother," Mrs. Harris said.

"That's right." I smiled like a child who has heard his name called out.

"Is he still alive?"

"Alive?"

"He was sick," she said.

"He was?"

"It's been a long time. I could be confused. How much older is he than you?"

"Five months."

"That's what I remember. Your parents told me he was sick."

"Very sick?"

"I don't know. The doctors couldn't agree on what was wrong, but they thought it might be something serious."

"My parents told you this?"

Mrs. Harris nodded. "Your parents fell in love with you. They'd already adopted your brother, but they weren't sure what would happen to him. I guess it was like insurance."

I got up from my seat and asked to be excused. I went into the bathroom and washed my face. I'd been a colicky baby, that I knew, but my parents hadn't told me I'd been sick. I listened to my pulse. It was steady. My lungs felt fine. Maybe I'd been born with a hole in my heart. It had happened to a girl in my nursery school. Born with a hole in her heart, she'd had to have emergency surgery. I could still hear my parents' voices: they'd adopted us both because each of us was beautiful. I looked at myself in the bathroom mirror. Had they adopted Jonathan to replace me?

When I came back to the table, Mrs. Harris was gone and our trays had been bussed. All I found was a napkin and on it a note:

Jonathan,

I was glad to meet you, but today has been too much for me. Take care of yourself. Make the most of your life. Know that I'll be thinking about you.

Rebecca Harris

Some people speak of a moment in their lives when everything changes. I've always been suspicious of such claims. They seem the product of retrospect, the urge to search for watersheds, to think of everything in terms of before and after, when in fact our lives are more haphazard than that and are made orderly only in the retelling.

But that day in the restaurant I changed my mind. I knew it the instant I read Mrs. Harris's note. It wasn't a case of getting what I'd hoped for—of information provided and curiosity put to rest. It was more than that. I realized what a fraud I'd been. I'd lied to Jenny, Jonathan, and Mrs. Harris; perhaps most of all I'd lied to myself—all in the hope of achieving something impossible, something I couldn't even put my hands on. My wish was as fanciful as the wish for time not to pass. I wanted my brother to be who he'd been years before; I wanted things to be the same between us. But I wasn't sure any longer what there had been between us—wasn't sure what was real and what I'd made up. The past year had been nothing but a string of lies: the lie that I was a Jew and that I wasn't a Jew, my parents' lying to me and my lying back, my identity slippery and slithering.

I hadn't realized this, but I might have searched for my birth father, despite what I'd told Susan. I might have disobeyed Mrs. Harris's order (had any such order ever stopped me?) and found Jonathan's brother and sister. There was no end to the searches I could have made if I was determined to make them. I'd hurt a lot of people. I didn't want to continue on this path. I'd have been happy not to know what I already knew. I haven't asked my parents whether I was sick as an infant, and I don't expect I ever will.

That evening, I ordered room service. At midnight on my nightstand lay a plate of scrambled eggs I hadn't eaten and a half-empty martini glass. I rarely drank, and I didn't feel like drinking now. But people were drinking in the movie on TV, and I was so lost I was imitating them, open to any suggestion.

Jenny hovered above me. I saw her next to Tara in the kitchen, the two of them doing their work. I didn't know why I wasn't with them, home where I belonged; didn't know what I was doing in this midwestern city, in a hotel room with a plastic card key in my jeans pocket, masquerading as someone I wasn't. I felt like a fool.

When I got home, Jenny wanted to know how the teachers' meeting had gone.

Of all the things that have happened between us, this is the most painful to recount. I had no choice but to lie to her, only now I was doing so without delusion.

If I'd told Jenny the truth, I believe she would have left me. I wouldn't have blamed her if she had. Perhaps I deserved to be left, but I was convinced we were on a new path, and I refused to sacrifice our relationship. I could say what you don't know can't hurt you, but I've never believed that was so. Someday I hope to tell Jenny the truth. Maybe I'll be able to tell Jonathan as well. For now I have to accept the lies I've told. They don't sit well with me.

Things improved between Jenny and me almost as soon as I got back. I can't say how, exactly, but I began to feel this was my life: Jenny and Tara; our home; my teaching; San Francisco itself. Everything felt less temporary and contingent. I neither looked to the past for phantom guidance nor avoided the future.

Jenny, in turn, must have sensed this. Our disagreements seemed less weighty. They were about what they were about, with less of a subtext. Jenny was more amenable to my spending time with Susan. Even my adoptees' support group didn't threaten her. It was a source of amusement more than anything else.

We got engaged a month later. I waited that long to bring the subject of marriage up because I wanted to be sure I wasn't doing this out of guilt, although I knew I wasn't. I'd been brought back to my senses just in time, thanks to Jenny's patience. All along I'd wanted to marry her. I can honestly say she saved me from myself; my life would be nothing without her.

Tara guessed our news before we could tell her. We must have had that marriage glow.

"How did you know?" Jenny asked.

"I just did. It was about time, don't you think?"

"Why?"

"Mom, you guys have been together for almost three years. How long were you going to just hang out?"

"Well, aren't you going to congratulate us?"

"Congratulations." Tara kissed Jenny, then me, on the cheek. She didn't sound enthusiastic, but it was unhip at her age to show any feelings about us other than amused embarrassment. I'd become part of the family. I could tell she was happy for us both. I think she was happy for herself also.

"Now will you finally let me go to boarding school?"

Jenny shook her head. "Ben and I need you around here. We'd be lonely without you."

Telling my parents, especially my father, was going to be more difficult. I called them to say Jenny and I were coming to New York and needed to talk to them.

"What's wrong?" my mother asked.

"Nothing. We just have something to tell you."

"We can play handball," my father said.

"Come on, Dad."

"Why not? I ride the stationary bike six days a week. I'm not so old."

I thought of him grading his blue books, a seventy-five-year-old man who still taught class, who came home at night and marked his papers, hunched over his desk now as always, the elbows of his jacket patched with suede, my father penciling in letters in the blue-book margins in secret Hebrew code.

We left Tara with a friend and flew to New York. When we got to my parents' apartment, my mother had lamb chops on the counter, ready to be broiled. Lamb chops used to be my favorite food, what I'd chosen every year for my birthday dinner. Sometimes my mother would call me "lamb chop" as she stroked my forehead before I went to sleep. She'd sit next to my father on the edge of the bed while he placed his hand like a yarmulke on my head and listened to me say the *shma*.

My mother and Jenny sliced radishes for the salad. I sat on the stool where I'd eaten breakfast as a child and listened to the sound of their knives against the cutting board. I thought maybe this wouldn't be as hard as I'd feared; maybe it wouldn't be so painful.

Jenny went to lie down before dinner. I set four places at the dining room table, then came back into the kitchen. My mother was making rice pilaf.

"I like Jenny," she said. "I hope you realize that."

"Thanks, Mom. I appreciate your saying it."

"Dad does too."

"I'm glad."

"Whatever you think about what we think, I hope you know we have nothing against her."

She seemed to understand why we were here, and was preparing for our announcement. Her hands fluttered like sparrows above the stove. She'd lost weight, I thought. For a moment I saw her like the skulls behind the window in my high school biology lab, becoming teeth and bone: my mother growing old on the heels of my father, osteoporitic and arthritic, with the cautious gait of the old women in Riverside Park careful not to slip on the ice.

"I know why you're here," my mother said.

I could tell she did. But I didn't want to talk about it. "Please, Mom, let's wait until Dad comes home."

She stirred the pilaf with a wooden spoon, her right hand moving in concentric circles, one after the other, wider and wider. Her hair hung in wisps above her eyes; a few strands were stuck to her forehead.

"I want to say something now," she said, "because when Dad is here it will be harder for me to say it."

"Okay."

"When you were small, I always told you that when you grew up, you and Jonathan could live as you wanted."

"We have."

"I know. Let me finish. I meant it then and I mean it now. But there was a time when I truly believed it wouldn't matter. I thought that as long as you were happy, one thing would be as good as the next."

"But it isn't?"

"It turns out to be more complicated. I know what you're thinking." She pointed at the adjoining sinks, one for milk and one for meat, then at the cabinet that held the sabbath candles and the unopened bottles of kiddush wine. "You wonder why this matters to me. You know how I grew up. God for me was 'The International.' I never thought I'd care about the Jewish laws."

"But?"

"But I've grown to." She untied her apron and set it down on the counter. It had "This Kitchen Is Kosher" written on it. Jonathan and I had bought it for her fortieth birthday. "In a way I still think these laws are archaic, and I don't believe in God. But over the years I've come to care about these things."

A pigeon walked along the window ledge. My mother hated the sounds pigeons made. During sabbath lunch she used to rap her slipper against the window and shoo them away. She looked down at the street. She had an intent expression on her face, as if something were staring back at her, some answer to a question she was trying to ask. "More than half my life I've been married to Dad. That's a lot of sabbaths together. Every time I cook a meal in this kitchen I'm aware of the kosher laws. He and I disagree about many things. But I've come to understand that Judaism is about continuity. Most religions are. By marrying Jenny—"

"Please, Mom. Don't try to preempt us."

"I'm not. I just want to explain what I'm feeling, and I want to do it now while I've got the chance. This is hard for Dad. I'm speaking for him because, although it's hard for me too, it's not as hard. And I don't think he'll be able to tell you this himself. This has nothing to do with Jenny. Both of us respect and admire her. We more than understand why you've fallen in love. I'm sorry we haven't welcomed her as much as you'd have liked—surely not as much as we should have. But that will change—from my side, I promise. From Dad's side too, I think, if you're patient enough."

I wouldn't have expected any different from her. She was my mother. I wanted to tell her I hadn't planned it this way; I'd have done anything not to disappoint her and my father. I wanted to tell her I still dreamed about them, my parents who had loved Jonathan and me and taken us in, who thought about us now, three thousand miles away, and still saw the babies they'd adopted.

We sat down to dinner when my father got home. My mother placed two lamb chops on everybody's plate and ladled portions of rice pilaf. In the living room the lamps were lit, casting shadows along the grand piano. I could see across the water, to where Palisades Amusement Park had once been. At night, Jonathan and I used to watch the roller coaster, the climb and dip of lights, a flash of color and then darkness.

Jenny sat across from me in Jonathan's old seat. My father sat opposite my mother. He was on the antique chair; it had lasted for twenty-eight years. Once when Jonathan and I were taking turns sitting on it, we accidentally chipped a piece off one arm. We woke up at three in the morning and secretly, fearfully, Krazy Glued the wood back together.

My father raised his wineglass in toast. "To seeing you, Ben."

"To seeing Jenny too," my mother said.

My father's shirtsleeves were rolled up. He was almost completely bald, and what hair he had was as white as the inside of a coconut. But the hair along his arms was still dark. I'd stroked those arms when I was a child, asking him to make a muscle for me, then feeling my own muscle. I'd asked him how much he weighed when he was my age, how tall he'd been at ten, how old he was when he started shaving. I wanted to know what to expect from my life; I was waiting to see what would happen. Jonathan and I: the only kids in the fourth grade who knew the meaning of the word *hirsute*. I used to wonder what my father's students thought about him, whether they compared themselves with him the way I did, whether in him they saw the unfolding of their world.

"I'm glad we're here," Jenny said.

"We're glad you're here too," said my mother.

"We have some news for you," Jenny said. We hadn't planned how we'd make the announcement. I assumed I'd tell my parents at dinner. But I realized now that Jenny was telling them. "Ben and I are getting married."

"Congratulations!" my mother said. She jumped out of her chair.

Her enthusiasm was so high-pitched it seemed almost willed. She hugged Jenny hard. Then she hugged me.

My father was quiet momentarily. His hands were so still on the table you might not have known he was alive. I'd seen movies in high school about fathers who said kaddish for their intermarried children. My father wouldn't do that. He was a reasonable man. But I wanted him to be happy for me, to be like the father I'd imagined he'd be on the day I told him I was getting married.

"Ben," he said. I thought he was going to remind me about the Millsteins. I could have sworn he started to say their name. "Congratulations."

But he wasn't happy. I wished this didn't hurt me so. He came over and kissed me on the forehead. He kissed Jenny on the forehead too. He laid his hands on Jenny's head and left them there for several seconds. In that moment, I allowed myself to believe he was blessing her. For that was how he'd looked blessing Jonathan and me on Friday nights, a time when I believed my father spoke to God, when anything he said he could make happen.

For our wedding, Jenny and I considered going to a justice of the peace, accompanied only by Tara. But we wanted the rest of our families to be there.

We planned a small wedding at Tilden Park, followed by lunch at Green's restaurant in Fort Mason.

"We're only inviting immediate family," I told my parents.

"And Susan, I assume," my mother said.

My mother might have liked a slightly larger wedding so that she could invite a few friends. But my father was content with something small. I suspect he would have preferred that Jenny and I elope—actually being at the ceremony would prove painful to him—although once we decided to have guests, he never considered refusing to come. We planned no Jewish content for the wedding, in part out of deference to him, but also because I wanted it that way. A Jewish wedding, I believe, takes place between two Jews. This may still be the Orthodoxy in me, but the God I knew as a child, whether or not He exists, wouldn't have wanted to be involved in this wedding, and I had no desire to involve Him.

My parents flew out two days before the wedding to meet Susan. I'd known this day would come, yet knowing it didn't make me any less nervous. I'd once had a fantasy about their meeting that amounted to a huge and joyous reunion, but I was long past wishing that would happen. I simply wanted them to get along.

I took Susan to my parents' hotel. I saw myself as a boxing referee, bringing the fighters to the center of the ring and demanding that they shake hands. But there was no hostility between them. Why should there have been? There was only the expected nervousness, no one sure what to do.

"Mom and Dad," I said when my parents came down to the lobby, "this is Susan Green." Then, as if anyone needed reminding, I said, "This is my birth mother."

My father shook Susan's hand. "I'm pleased to meet you again."

"I am too," said Susan.

"We're happy you'll be joining us at the wedding," my mother told her.

"I wouldn't miss it for the world."

I wasn't worried about my father. But Susan can be voluble when she gets nervous, and my mother, when threatened, can turn snobbish and make such an occasion unpleasant. Having Susan find me was hard for both my parents, but I've come to realize that it was more difficult for my mother simply because Susan was also my mother and therefore in direct competition with her.

"I'm glad Ben's getting married," Susan said. "Jenny's terrific."

"Yes, she is," my father said. "Ben's mother and I are both very fond of her."

"We love her," said my mother. My parents seemed to be trying to outdo Susan with their declarations of affection for their new daughter-in-law.

Suddenly Susan said, "Ben looks like you."

"Like who?" said my mother.

"You."

My mother seemed unsure whether Susan was making fun of her.

"I mean it," Susan said. "These things probably happen over time. You begin to look like the people you live with."

My mother's not one to be easily flattered, but in these circumstances she was.

"You clearly were good parents," Susan said. "No one turns out like Ben because of good luck."

My mother reached out as if to touch Susan's hand, then thought better of it and pulled back.

"He had good genes too," my father said. "That counts for a lot."

Susan smiled in gratitude. Everyone was being polite to the point of exaggeration. *He's wonderful because of you. . . . No, because of you.*

My father said, "Ben probably told you that we lied to him about his having been born Jewish."

"Yes," Susan answered.

"Well, it was a mistake, and we regret it. I just want you to know we didn't do it out of hostility to you or your religion."

"I understand. I never thought you did."

"We just wanted to make things easier for Ben, although I realize now that we probably made them harder."

My mother brought back four cups of coffee from a machine. "We heard about your son," she told Susan. "We're very sorry."

"I appreciate it," Susan said.

"No one should have to go through that." My mother's voice was loud and emphatic.

The three of them grew quiet. The thought of Scottie's death appeared to unite them. They'd all been parents, and they knew what every parent knows—that nothing is more awful than the death of one's child.

"I want to thank you for making things easier for me," Susan said.

"How do you mean?" my mother asked.

"You haven't interfered in my relationship with Ben. Scottie can never be replaced, but getting to know Ben has been very important to me."

"We should thank you too," my father said. "You gave him to us, after all."

I had the odd feeling of not being there—the impresario of this reunion, the focus of this conversation, who had, however, receded.

"Tell me something," my mother said, "did you ever regret giving Ben up?"

This question startled me. I saw no purpose to it other than to upset Susan. Perhaps it was a lapse in my mother's judgment. Although I think she was hoping Susan would say no. My mother didn't want to feel bad for having taken me from Susan.

"What's done is done," Susan said. The cliché made me cringe. But it also summed up what had happened between us, everything I felt right then.

Jenny and I got married in Tilden Park on a beautiful Sunday in March. We stood on a hill and said our vows in front of the justice of the peace. Jonathan took out a glass for me to step on. I was touched that he'd thought of this Jewish tradition. I turned toward my father, who made no motion to object. I trusted that God—whoever He was, wherever He was—would allow me this connection to my people.

I smashed the glass with my foot. In the quiet of the Berkeley hills, Jonathan shouted, "*Mazel tov!*"

Jenny and I kissed. She'd opted for a straw hat instead of a veil, which tipped over as she leaned into me. Laughter rose and then subsided. We kissed long and hard. We were alone, it seemed. Jenny's knees pressed against my shins. Her dress billowed behind her in the breeze.

When the ceremony was over, we mingled with our families. My parents had met Jenny's only an hour before the wedding, and now they were talking to each other. I'd been so focused on my parents' meeting Susan that I hadn't paid much attention to my new in-laws. They felt almost incidental, as if Susan were the new parent I was welcoming to the family.

Later, while we all ate lunch, I remembered a bar mitzvah I'd gone to at the Pierre in New York. The bar mitzvah boy wore a velvet suit and had his name printed on the after-dinner mints. It was a lavish affair, which my parents didn't approve of, but I loved the feel of velvet against my hands and wanted to have a bar mitzvah like that.

My parents refused.

"It's a waste of money," my father said.

"At your wedding," my mother said, "if you still care about these things, you can wear as many velvet suits as you like."

I wondered whether my parents remembered that now. It's funny looking back at what we once argued about—a velvet suit, names on mints—when everything that's happened since then has been so much weightier and more difficult.

I remembered what my father had begun to say when Jenny and I announced our engagement. He seemed to want to remind me about the Millsteins.

For this was the end of my father's story. Peter Millstein married the Swedish girl from the kibbutz, and for a while they were happy, for a while things went well. But a while, my father said, doesn't make a lifetime. Peter, who thought he didn't care about being Jewish, slowly began to feel like a Jew. He went back to synagogue and learned Hebrew. He started to celebrate the Jewish holidays. He looked at his children, who knew nothing about being Jewish, and wondered why he'd thought he didn't care.

It's hard to know why Peter got divorced, but the Millsteins had an idea. They looked at the portrait of Golda Meir, which still hung on the wall in their living room. They thought about the trees they'd planted in the Negev. They couldn't read Hebrew; they went to synagogue just on Yom Kippur. But they felt Jewish, and so did their son. Sometimes a feeling runs so deep it's inside you without your even knowing it.

I would have listened to my father repeat his story. I'd have stared up at the Hebrew books that lined the shelves, the volumes of the Torah and Talmud, all those words he'd hoped would protect me.

And I would have said, "But the Millsteins aren't real."

"To me they are," he would have said.

And I'd have understood him.

I had no illusions, I would have told him, my father who said marriage was more than love, who said it was shared history and culture, who taught me years ago about my *bashert,* until I believed that she'd been picked for me by God, that she was floating in the air like those molecules we'd learned about in science class. I'd have told my father I stood by my decision; I loved Jenny and we were going to make a life.

During my spring break, Jenny and I set out on a short honeymoon, camping in Glacier National Park. Tara stayed home with a babysitter. The day before we left, Susan came over to say good-bye to me. She handed me an envelope. Inside was a check for three thousand dollars.

"I can't accept this," I told her.

"It's your wedding gift. May you have only happiness."

"Susan, this is way too much money."

"Think of it as the violin lessons I never paid for, or as eighteen years of back allowance."

"You're leaving, right?" I wasn't sure how I knew this. I just did. "You're flying home to your husband."

Susan nodded. "We're going to try to work things out."

That was what I'd wanted. It was part of the reason I'd written Frank. So why were there tears in my eyes?

I forced myself to laugh. "Look at me, I'm crying."

"I'll be back to visit. Besides, you can always come see me in Indiana."

"What about your earrings? The stores in San Francisco that sell your work?"

"Ben," she said, "a person isn't the sum of her accomplishments."

I realized then what I should have all along, what I suspect I did realize. There were no stores selling her earrings. She'd come to San Francisco simply to see me but had been too embarrassed to admit it. For all I knew, she didn't make earrings. The one I'd found in her apartment might have been made by someone else. She'd become a part of me. Even if I never saw her again, I'd count her as a friend. In ways that are too complicated to express, she has changed my life. But sometimes I think I will never know her—never know what was the truth and what were lies. Some people might say the same about me. Although, at core, I consider myself honest. The boy who walked the rest of the way to school instead of reusing his bus pass is still lodged within me.

"I'll miss you," I said.

"I'll miss you too."

The tears came again. "What is it about me? I've never learned how to say good-bye."

I took Susan to the door and watched her descend the stairs. I stood at the window facing the street, my nose pressed to the glass as she walked away.

I saw my parents three months later. Summer had come, and my mother was redecorating the apartment. She wanted Jonathan and me to clear out our old bedrooms.

We found things we should have thrown away years before: school IDs, autograph books, Dairylea milk coupons good for New York Mets tickets, a notebook from the year we started taking Spanish with the words "I hate French" scrawled in the margins. I found my high school basketball uniform and decided to keep it; maybe I'd have a son who'd want to wear it. Or maybe I'd give it to Tara.

We came across the books my parents had read us. *Horton Hears a Who. Pierre. Where the Wild Things Are. Are You My Mother?*

"Here's *The Story of Babar*," Jonathan said. He held the book open on his lap. My mother had read it to us, always skipping the same page so we wouldn't know Babar's mother dies. I felt a touch of sadness at giving these books away; Jonathan clearly did also.

Saturday night, when the sabbath was over, my father said *havdala*. We smelled the spices and closed our eyes, waiting for the new week to begin.

"We can check the smoke alarm," Jonathan said.

My mother smiled. "The smoke alarm's doing fine."

"You never know," I told her.

I flipped the lights on and off, the way I'd done as a child to celebrate the end of sabbath restrictions.

Then we all went into my parents' bedroom. My father opened the file cabinets across the room; my mother stood next to him.

"Everything's here." He ran his hand over the papers.

"All the important records," she said.

I'd known there were records in the cabinets, but I'd never given any thought to them. They were mostly tax documents, I'd supposed. My parents didn't own any property; they still rented their apartment. They had some stocks and bonds, but I didn't know what they'd invested in or how much these investments were worth.

"Here's a copy of our wills." My mother touched her finger to a sealed manila envelope, then drew it back quickly, as though the paper were hot.

"You should know where they are," my father said.

"I've drawn up a living will," said my mother.

It was as if my parents were on their deathbeds, leaving us instructions about what to do.

"I don't want to be resuscitated," she said. "No heroic measures. No excessive pain. No being kept alive as a vegetable."

"I understand," I said.

"Dad feels differently. He's willing to put up more of a fight."

Maybe it was because he was religious and believed God would decide when it was time for him to die. Or maybe it was because he didn't feel pain. That's what I'd imagined when I was a boy, when I pictured him in World War II, hiking twenty-five miles carrying a rifle and a backpack, thinking about nothing but beating the Germans, holed up in the bunkers reciting poetry.

The next day, my father took Jonathan and me to the cemetery in New Jersey where his parents were buried. Although he visited their graves every year, Jonathan and I hadn't been there since the funerals, almost twenty-five years before. My father wanted us to come along.

He stood at his father's tombstone with his head bowed. He was seventy-five and his shoulders were stooped, but to me he was the man who'd shagged fly balls with me, Cleon Jones to my Tommie Agee, who never was as happy as when I turned sixteen and finally beat him in four-wall handball.

He kissed the ground beside his parents' tombstones. Jonathan and I followed his lead.

All three of us stood up. My father had tears in his eyes. He looked at us and shrugged. *"Adam yisodo may'afar vi'sofo le'afar."*

Man is made from dust and returns to dust.

"I'll be buried here," he said.

I'd never heard him say this before, never heard him admit he was going to die. It scared me to hear it, as if his saying it would make it happen, as if, suddenly, he'd given up the fight.

"You're still young," I said.

He smiled. "You're right. Forty-five more years until I'm a hundred and twenty."

I looked around me. New Jersey was just miles from where I'd grown up, but I'd spent so little time there it felt more like an idea, a state writ large by my imagination.

"I have a plot for myself," my father said, "and a plot for Mom. We can get plots for you guys too, if you'd like. We can all be buried together."

"I want to be buried with Jenny," I said.

"We can get a plot for her as well."

Jenny couldn't be buried in a Jewish cemetery. Was it possible my father had forgotten?

"Sandy too," he told my brother.

I wanted to ask him to get a plot for Susan, as if it mattered, as if you were anything but dead when you died. I'd once learned that when the Messiah comes all Jews go to Israel, the dead as well as the living, and that the farther you are from Israel the harder the trip, the longer the distance your bones have to roll.

"I'm not going to die," Jonathan said.

"Good," my father said. "I'm not either."

If you prepare for the worst, he'd told us once, maybe it won't happen. He'd been talking about mundane things—studying for school, buying car insurance—but now I realized it was a general principle. It was why he'd shown us his will and why he was talking about burial plots. He was looking death in the eye. He would live forever, he was telling us. For an instant I let myself believe it.

I stared at him standing at his father's tombstone, my grandfather and not my grandfather, a bearded man from Eastern Europe whom I hadn't known well but whose picture I'd studied. I'd convinced myself I looked like him. I stood next to Jonathan in that graveyard in New Jersey and watched my father whisper to the dead, his pants legs flapping in the wind as he turned back to face us.